D1564236

Hebe Uhart

ANIMALS

TRANSLATED FROM THE SPANISH BY
Robert Croll

archipelago books

Library of Congress Cataloging-in-Publication Data available upon request.

Archipelago Books
232 3rd Street #A111
Brooklyn, NY 11215
www.archipelagobooks.org

Distributed by Penguin Random House
www.penguinrandomhouse.com

Cover art by Hebe Uhart

This work was made possible by the New York State Council on the Arts
with the support of Governor Andrew M. Cuomo and the New York State
Legislature. Funding for the translation of this book was provided
by a grant from the Carl Lesnor Family Foundation.

This publication was made possible with support from Lannan Foundation,
the National Endowment for the Arts, and the New York City
Department of Cultural Affairs.

This work has been published within the framework of the Sur Translation
Support Programme of the Ministry of Foreign Affairs, International
Trade and Worship of the Argentine Republic.
Obra editada en el marco del Programa Sur de Apoyo a las
Traducciones del Ministerio de Relaciones Exteriores, Comercio
Internacional y Culto de la República Argentina.

Printed in Canada

ANIMALS

Contents

[All illustrations drawn by the author]

DUSKY HAWK

My History with Animals

M Y FATHER used to enjoy confusing the children. He would sing: "Of all the many birds that fly, I like the pig." My response to this song was first suspicion, then annoyance. When I was about six years old, he'd take me on walks around the outskirts of Moreno, which already turned to countryside only eight blocks from downtown, and the plumpest cows stood out there behind wire fences. He would tell me:

"Say hello."

And I would say:

"Hello there, cow."

If one of them mooed, he would tell me:

"See? Now she's saying hello."

Around the same period, we used to go over on Sundays to eat at my uncle and aunt's retreat in Paso del Rey, where my grandmother lived. The place was enormous but more rustic than my house. There were instructions about which things were off limits: I mustn't chase after the hens, mustn't sit in the chairs on the little patio as they could be rather dirty, mustn't touch Milonga the dog too much. Milonga didn't belong to anyone; he was part of the place and came and went with total autonomy, without anyone sparing him a glance. But I liked to pet him, and I'd sit on the ground while he stood by my side, at peace.

"He's a street dog!" they'd tell me.

I didn't understand the difference between street dogs and house dogs, just as I didn't understand the difference between wild and cultivated flowers; for me, those tiny flowers that look identical to daisies belonged to the same family; my mother called them *flores de bicho colorado*, red mite flowers. A few years later, when I was around nine, my mother sent me on a bus to Paso del Rey to visit Aunt María, whose house stood next door to my other aunt and uncle's holiday home; they used to bring food for her. I brought María whatever she asked for from Moreno: Rachel face powder, hairpins, and a wonderful scented soap. Why she requested these things I'll never know; her long white hair hung down past her shoulders, the dress she wore was totally threadbare, and she kept chickens, shut up inside a little room (that felt like a place for storing junk) so that they wouldn't mingle with the chickens from my aunt and uncle's coop. She'd only let them out on very rare occasions when she fancied it. When these chickens of hers did get out, they were all crooked and unsteady, unable to walk right. She did bathe a few of them; they were clearly wasting away, but she didn't appear to acknowledge the fact. I'd always known she was off her rocker and accepted that, but by age seven or so I wondered how it could be, given her state, that plants sprouted for her just the same as they did for others. She had a nice yard and even kept a sweetbriar rose, but I never caught her watering a thing. The plants there were a little more unkempt than those in other gardens, but I used to think that, since she acted this way, so peculiar, she ought to have plants befitting her condition, weird plants. Rain was common there, and I thought it must have been a different sort of rain to suit her. Going there to bring her the powder and soap was slightly unnerving for me, since she received me warmly sometimes but other times kicked me out, calling me a "gossip," which was true, of course, since I'd go back to Moreno and tell my mom about all the goings-on around there. I now suspect they were sending me as a spy.

However perplexing this errand was, there was something nice about taking the bus to Paso del Rey on my own. But on the way into María's house there was a little rustic wooden door, and behind that door lay the southern screamer. A southern screamer is like a kind of giant lapwing with large wing spurs; this one was always idling around by that little door. I took my precautions before passing through the doorway, taking the long way round and never getting too close for fear of setting off its spurs. I know now that they can fly; it's a good thing I didn't know back then, or I never would've made it through. How the creature came to be there, I couldn't say, for my aunt never gave it a glance or a name, being indifferent to the yard and the plants. In any case, I always thought the southern screamer was a fitting animal for my aunt; such a thing could never have lived at my house. Aunt María called Milonga the dog "milord," as though exalting his name, and it's quite strange to think of her calling him that, as I don't believe she was aware of the existence of lords.

. . . . . .

When I was around ten years old, my father was given a pony, but I have scarcely any memory of the animal. We lived in a village house, with a glass outer door and a large patio with a garden all the way around. On the morning after the pony's arrival, a "tucutún, tucutún" could be heard out beyond the patio. My mother went out to look. The pony had gotten loose because my father had only tied it with sisal twine. Since Moreno was a town whose inhabitants were almost all of rural origins, she said:

"But what an idea! Where was this man raised?"

She often said things like that. The pony disappeared that very morning.

. . . . . .

I can't recall having invoked animals for insults, but all sorts have been called upon in insulting ways. "Dog" is there in the *Iliad*; "eyes of a dog," they say. They used to call a girl in my sixth-grade class "the horse," and hookers "cats," and fat women "cows." I identify with Felisberto Hernández in his story "Úrsula," when he says, "Úrsula was fat as a cow and I liked her that way." It takes a bit of courage to say that in Río de la Plata. "Forked tongue" is another insult; "vulture" too. Tigers, lions, and sheep get better press. I quite like the folk sayings from around Buenos Aires, in which all situations, all skills or shortcomings, are illustrated by way of animals. For monotony: "Always the same, like a sheep's expression." For seriousness: "Formal as a donkey in the corral." For suspicion: "Less trusting than a one-eyed horse." For people who talk about things they know nothing about: "What does that ass know about candy, he's never owned a candyshop." For people who say hello to everyone in town: "He greets you like a lapwing." (Lapwings make a nodding movement with their heads, wobbling as they peer in every direction.) My father used to point out how the old Basques in the country had animal nicknames: "Bay horse," "Pinto," "Blaze."

At age twelve I entered first year and went to study in Buenos Aires, in a very urban world. My secondary school was quite large, with something like eight divisions of first-year girls, and I was frightened by the number of children out at recess, by the strict discipline, and by etiquette in general. For me, etiquette was related to the idea that no one ever looked at you, nor could you take a good look at those girls and their chaperones. (I was already familiar with Buenos Aires because we'd go there once a month, more or less, dressed up in white gloves; I'd always lose one and try not to let my aunt notice, for she was the family's arbiter of elegance; she'd take her time to bring me to a shop-front carousel, where I'd watch legs upon legs of people passing, and then we'd go to La Ideal for tea and pastries, though she'd only let me eat two, for any more than that was gluttony.)

But in my second year, a zoology teacher came, and—not out of any interest in zoology, much less insects—I studied everything she cared to teach. As soon as she introduced herself in the first lesson, she set about teaching without saying any of the sorts of things that others would declare, things like "hard work will be rewarded," nor did she mention unit one, a description of what zoology was and what would be covered, the same thing that's described in unit one of every subject, both here and on Mars, to the boredom and dismay of the respective inhabitants. She set about teaching us the orders of insects, and I can remember some even now: Diptera, Coleoptera, Orthoptera, Hymenoptera; I studied the insects orders as if my life depended on it, because I loved her. Whenever she turned around to draw a beautiful coleoptera on the blackboard, using colored chalks that she kept hidden inside a little box she carried with her, I saw the expanse of her flat, washbasin rear end, which accentuated her image of benevolence. There was nothing in her appearance that called attention; her clothing was ordinary, she applied lipstick sensibly, and she was heavy but that wasn't what stood out at first. She produced a kind of calm, a restraint. And that's what made me study, in the afternoons, on the patio where the pony had once run off in its confusion: Diptera, Coleoptera, Orthoptera, Hymenoptera.

. . . . . .

Once, I saw a girl in Río de Janeiro carrying what they call a finger monkey. He could fit right inside the palm of your hand, and she had him riding on her shoulder; he looked like an angry little man, his fur standing up like a brush. She sparked a great envy in me, as if the life she led was fuller and happier than my own. And now I'm always seeing dog walkers on the street, and it amazes me how they keep their charges so well arranged, one beside the next. I'm not sure whether it's done by size, closeness with the leader, or elective affinities among the dogs. I like the role these people serve; they're animal collectors (they go along picking them up from their houses) and animal educators as well. The other day, a walker went by, saying to one dog: "I've already told you a thousand times. This is the last time I'm going to say it." And it is for all of these reasons that I place myself, among the characters illustrated by Theophrastus, disciple of Aristotle, with The Boor. Of this archetype, he says: "Nothing awakens his admiration or startles him on the streets so much as the sight of an ox, an ass, or a goat, and then he stands agape in contemplation." I do the same.

The Ostrich

WHEN ONE of those strands of cobweb known as devil's drool finds its way onto my balcony, or when I come across a snail or a lizard among the plants, I become aware that this plain was once entirely populated by birds and giant tortoises and enormous monsters. One of these birds was the giant ostrich, which went extinct around six thousand years ago and from which descends our rhea, called a *surí* in the north of the country and a *choique* in the south. Ours are relatives of the larger African ostrich and the emu, still greater in size. All members of this family agree on several points: in all pairs the males incubate the eggs, and all can kick with great strength but are unable to fly due to the great weight of their bodies. Aelian, a writer from the second century, says: "The Ostrich is covered with thick feathers, but its nature does not permit it to rise from the ground and mount aloft into the sky. Yet its speed is very great, and when it

RHEA

spreads its wings on either side, the wind meeting them causes them to belly like sails." Hudson called it "ship of the wilderness." They can run at sixty kilometers per hour, changing the position of their wings as they go, alternately lowering one after the other and then lifting both. This form of running, along with the fact that they can't fly, has sparked the curiosity of ornithologists; it's as if they wonder: how can we understand a species that isn't able to fly? The perplexity it spurs is similar to that regarding the size of the toucan's beak. Darwin wondered what the purpose of such an enormous bill could be.

These creatures have an air of being out of place; maybe, still accustomed to being giants, they don't feel comfortable among the little birds of the plains. They seem stupid but but must not be, since they've endured for so long, and their stomachs can hold up against nails and wire: they eat everything they see. The Mexican writer Juan José Arreola said of the ostrich: "It suffers from an absolute lack of grace." No one thinks of them as beautiful or useful, but they can manage on their own. Clemente Onelli, a former director of the Buenos Aires Zoo, tells of how they kept an African ostrich in 1905. To find a mate for him, they chose native rheas, which are much smaller (and they made them walk before him in single file like a lineup of models because that was how the keepers in Algeria mated them). And the African ostrich would not choose a single one and sent them all away with a kick. They kick out to the right and left because they have few other defensive strategies; the caracaras steal their young, flying in little crisscrossing swoops to distract them. Armadillos will steal them as well, tunneling right up to their nests.

Here in Buenos Aires, the indigenous people used to hunt rheas to make feather plumes, which they would sell in Plaza Once around 1820. And natives in the Chaco would hunt them by dressing up to look like rheas themselves. And all of this interest I find in rheas comes from the stories told by María, the pedicurist; when she lived in the country in Corrientes, the rhea was a regular customer on the patio at her house. That bird would eat everything, including the assignments that the teacher had given them. And when a child said, "Miss, I couldn't bring my homework," the teacher would already know and answer, "Sure, I know, the rhea ate it."

The Meerkat

AMONG ALL CREATURES, the one I find most intriguing is the meerkat. If a meerkat still has its ears, it keeps them flat against its head, and the animal looks as if its head and body had been formed from one single block, as if it had been thought up all at once in a fit of inspiration. I have a sense that their perception works in the same way, that their bodies accompany those alert eyes entirely. I can't imagine them yawning or distracted; wherever they lay their eyes, they lay their understanding, and wherever they lay understanding, they lay their bodies. They're constantly looking off to the right and left, rotating their heads in a motion that the gym teacher might recommend for stretching your neck, a single elastic movement, and although they have one "official" lookout, all of the others remain on constant vigil as well; when there's danger, they form a line and look like the idols on Easter Island. They never exhibit doubt or hesitation. (They may well be dogmatists.) To all appearances, meerkats are charming, and yet they belong to a society that has terrible rules with regard to courtship; a young male must look outside his own community to find a mate and must then avoid being seen by the males from that other community, for if they see him, they'll kill him. As pedagogues, they do quite well, and most often it isn't the mother but an unmated aunt who teaches the baby meerkat to dig; they dig for scorpions, and before the baby catches one, the aunt will remove its stinger. They chew away as if they had mechanical jaws, and in this way the teacher demonstrates the recommended process for proper digestion, scrupulously chewing up all the food herself. The meerkat gets along well (so they say) with the drongo (an African bird) because these birds will give warning when there's danger from an eagle, yet there they are in the Kalahari, digging some holes, and a drongo signals false danger from an eagle and then steals a meerkat's food; when a bird tries this ploy for the second time during the day, the meerkats don't fall for it. Drongos have also learned to imitate the meerkats' calls, but they only deceive them during the summer, when food grows scarce, remaining the best of friends in winter. The drongos come to act like the police, sometimes protecting the people and sometimes taking from them.

The meerkats dig away at top speed, and, given their eager way of doing everything quickly and without thinking, along with the fact that their default seems to be to work in ensemble, I have an urge to set music to them, as if they lived on a stage. No doubt, when a baby meerkat is dead tired, it will literally flop down onto the ground, stretched out to its full length.

Aelian, On the Nature of Animals

IN ANCIENT THOUGHT, an important idea was the final cause, that is, the reason why something is done or whom it is done for. It's interesting to look at how this concept took shape. Just as we, in all our actions, make use of a means to arrive at an end (we pick up a knife in order to cut, I work to earn money, I go to the shop, etc.) the final cause was applied to broader and vaguer matters such as, for example, why are we here in this world? For the Greeks, the answer was "in order to fulfill our rational nature." In Christian thought, we are here in order to love and serve God. But people have also wondered why there are animals in this world, and, apart from their existing in service of man for his use, some have considered that they must be here to provide examples of fidelity, moderation, and so forth. In Christian parables, there are several examples of virtuous plants and animals: "Consider the lilies of the field, how they grow; they toil not, neither do they spin" (and intention should be added to that as well; they do not plot evil deeds). And even Saint Augustine says, regarding sex among elephants: "Observe the elephants, what restraint they show in sex, for they only mate every five or six years and always for the purpose of procreation."

Animals and plants exist in this world to serve as examples to us. Aelian, a second-century writer, makes a curious synthesis of information and moral didacticism in his work *On the Nature of Animals*. Both from observation and from a wide range of accounts, he knows the habits of various animals. Some of his descriptions share a kinship with those of current zoologists; for example, he describes the song of the partridge, which is variable according to region, just as today's ornithologists speak of birds' dialects, which change by region. Another corroboration from modern times is the bond that birds can form to human beings, something Aelian recorded, although he also speaks of a viper falling in love . . . with a man. Mind you, according to him, they'll only fall in love with beautiful people. Animal intelligence was already known of long ago, for example that of dolphins, which he points out when describing how they were of assistance to fishermen. But sometimes he goes too far, and he doesn't hesitate to assert that lions can understand the language of the Moors. (The premise of something like this happening among the Moors must be owed in part to the presence of some skeptic among his audience and in part to the idea that in distant and exotic parts there occurred things never seen in this land.) He says that the owl resembles a witch, for it can cast an enchantment upon its captors, and that of all the animals on earth the jackal is the closest friend to man, for if one crosses paths with a human, it will give way in deference.

One example: "The Octopus feeds first on one thing and then on another, for it is terribly greedy and forever plotting some evil."

And as for their predilections, he projects notions of status: "It is chiefly a mare with a long mane that is so full of airs and graces. For instance, she scorns to be covered by an ass, but is glad to mate with a horse, regarding herself as only fit for the greatest *of her kind*." Of the Ibis, the sacred bird of Egypt, he says: "Of its own free will the Ibis would never quit Egypt . . . It walks quietly like a maiden, and one would never see it moving at anything faster than a foot's pace." An example of fine manners.

About the raven, he says: "Of the Raven you might say that it has a spirit no less daring than the eagle, for it even attacks animals, and not the smallest either, but asses and bulls." He also says of the raven: "The Raven must really be the most clamorous of birds and have the largest variety of tones, for it can be taught to speak like a human being. For playful moods it has one voice, for serious moods another, and if it is delivering answers from the gods, then its voice assumes a devout and prophetic tone." That is, the raven was perceived as an unusual bird, more expressive than others; today, there are studies being conducted regarding their intelligence.

Of the crow, he says: "Crows are exceedingly faithful to each other, and when they enter into partnership they love one another intensely, and you would never see these creatures indulging freely in promiscuous intercourse. And those who are accurately informed about them assert that if one dies, the other remains in widow-hood." Of a bird called the purple coot, he says: "It is violent in its jealousy and keeps a close watch on the mated female birds, and if it discovers the mistress of its house to be adulterous, it strangles itself." The seal: "The Seal, I am told, vomits up the curdled milk from its stomach so that epileptics may not be cured thereby. Upon my word the Seal is indeed a malignant creature."

This attribution of purposefulness and above all kinship between the seal and a being as distant to it as an epileptic human reveals that the author thinks someone is orchestrating the animals in order to provide us examples of justice, forbearance, and even wickedness. What he says about lions is priceless:

"If the master of the house . . . is out and his wife is left all alone, then with words that put the Lion to shame she checks his approach . . . The Lion, it seems, understands the Moorish tongue; and the sense of the rebuke which the woman administers to the animal is (so they say) as follows. 'Are not you ashamed, you, a Lion, the king of beasts, to come to my hut and to ask a woman to feed you, and do you, like some cripple, look to a woman's hands hoping that thanks to her pity and compassion you may get what you want?—You who should be on your way to mountain haunts in pursuit of deer and antelopes and all other creatures that lions may eat without discredit. Whereas, like some sorry lap-dog, you are content to be fed by another.' Such are the spells she employs, whereupon the Lion, as though his heart smote him and he were filled with shame, quietly and with downcast eyes moves off, overcome by the justice of her words."

This reference to the lion's behavior relates to the idea that in wondrous lands events occur as befits that context, but it's clear that even Aelian does not find this so believable himself, for he explains, by way of justifying his claim, that the Moors raise lions as domestic animals and the cubs drink milk right beside their own children.

Aelian is the Animal Planet of his time.

SCARLET FLYCATCHER

The Ecopark

I ARRIVE QUITE EARLY at the Buenos Aires Zoo, which they've turned into an ecological park. It doesn't open until ten, and so I go out for breakfast; the street is full of human animals. (That's the right way to say it now, for if you were to say "human beings," you would be implying an offense toward animals, regarding them as non-human beings.) The human animal has constructed sheds for its mash, feed, and water; these are the cafés and restaurants where we all gather for breakfast. Everyone needs a bit of mash to eat. At a table next to mine, a very elderly pair of human animals is having breakfast. The female talks at great length to the male, who picks up the newspaper from time to time. Suddenly, he says:

"Look, if you're going to go on talking about diseases, why don't you call a taxi and go home?"

He sent her away from the trough. She made a loop and must

have gone to the bathroom but then sat down with him again. I'm not sure what they could have said at that point, but they looked happy, laughing.

And now it's time to go to the zoo. The place has been transformed into an ecopark, and some of the animals are at liberty, for example the maras (Patagonian hares), which are all over the place, walking peacefully among the humans with a parading step. The peacocks walk around freely inside their enclosure, the plumes on their heads recalling Comechingón headdresses. One, running loose, is pompous but has the goods to back it up, his tail sweeping the ground; he is parrot green in color, then blue, gold. Colors adored by the Greeks. Next door there are a few black ducks, floating along as if weightless, but their little legs are visible in motion through the water, and below the surface their feet look like tiny spiders.

The vultures' parcel of land is full of beautiful plants, but I'm not sure they deserve it; it must be an inheritance from their wealthy relative, the condor. The condor is indeed a kind of vulture. The vultures have several scraps of meat on the ground, and some crouch atop their pieces to defend them.

There are very few monkeys out and about, as the rest are away in quarantine or something like that, and only the spider monkey is in sight. A park ranger tells me: "We call him Punga, pickpocket, because he steals food from the birds, and when there are lots of people gathered around, he'll put on a show, running up and down that little staircase."

There are two elephants, but they're so old and inert that it's unclear whether they're a couple, or minerals, or a nightmare apparition. The female elephant stares at me, collects a bit of soil with her trunk, and swallows it; her tail is tattered and looks like a homemade broom, one of the kind they call *pichanilla* brooms up north.

By contrast, the meerkats are brimming with activity; one of them gives a plastic ball a headbutt, then another rolls it along with a paw, while another looks on with a severe expression; they have the look of a hardworking people. A strict but loving family; suddenly the three tangled bodies formed a single ball.

Nearby, a sign reads: "Flamingos from southern Chile." They're all crowded together on a distant shore of the lake, quite far from the people, at the other end of the range of hills. There are also ostriches of various sizes, the African ostrich, large, and the lesser rhea, small. The bigger the ostrich, the more foolish it seems, the long neck ending in a tiny head that looks too small for its body. The ostrich eats by poking his head inside a hut that looks like a postal box. He's in with the doves, who have no difficulty mating, whereas the male ostrich tried to start something with the female, but she turned him down. He treads with his whole foot when he walks; he must be flat-footed. A man among the spectators gives the right sort of whistle, and the rhea lifts his foolish little head.

The giraffe's house is ugly and has the look of a run-down castle; mother and child are rubbing up against each other, head to head.

There aren't many animals, but on the other hand there are a great many monuments, pagodas, shrines, cupolas, and sculptures. By the entrance, an inscription says: "Discover the architectural and cultural heritage of the park." In reality, it should be called Zoo Museum instead of Ecopark, because all those sculptures and palazzos, which really are worth seeing, are more valuable as an expression of how a zoo was conceived in the nineteenth century.

Why should these animals live among castles, monuments, and palazzos? There's a statue of Bacchus, for example; they can't drink wine. Another of these restored sculptures is the Temple of Vesta (a shrine to virgins), yet what's the sense in that, if they don't practice celibacy? Still, there was one monument I liked, the mausoleum of Clemente Onelli. It has an inscription: "A hard-working and progressive scholar, he loved this place as he loved his homeland." To the left of the bust is a bas-relief depicting a man and a woman, and to the right a chimpanzee petting a baby monkey.

From the Ecopark, a half-zoo even now, a great commotion can be seen on the grounds of La Rural, across the way, where the grenadiers are playing *Aurora* on horseback. Will the spider monkey climb up his staircase to spy out over all the commotion? What will he perceive? Outside, the human animals are all in motion; there go the Colorados del Monte, for example, with their horses and red ponchos. (They come from La Plata.) Other human animals on bicycles ride on the sidewalk to avoid traffic. While in line for the bus that will take me home, I talk to a woman from Paraguay, who, like everyone else, has been waiting a long time for any bus to turn up: they're slow to come. The woman says to me:

"We're stuck here waiting and waiting while they drink yerba mate."

Which is only a bit of grass.

Life in the Woods

I was reading a book by Thoreau: *Walden; or, Life in the Woods*. Thoreau was born in 1817 and died at the age of forty-four. He was a poet and thinker, with a philosophy close to anarchism. (He was once jailed after refusing to pay his taxes for ideological reasons, believing that the state weighed too heavily on the lives of the people.) He built a cabin with his own two hands on a plot of land given to him by his greatly admired Emerson, who also paid the fine for his civil disobedience. The book is an unsettling one: at times I find Thoreau a bit mad, but after reading other things I find him quite right. He fought against the plundering of nature for the sake of progress, something that he believed often existed in name only; he considered so much consumption unnecessary, found the inheritance of assets to be an excess, and doubted the idea that age grants wisdom.

Thoreau read Homer, Ovid, and Hindu philosophers, and he

bathed in the pond and rose early in keeping with Vedic thought, which says that intelligence awakens in the morning and that "to affect the quality of the day, that is the highest of arts." He could ignore the newspapers because they didn't bring any important news; all the news in them was gossip. When the floor of his shack was dirty, he would take all the pieces of furniture outside and contemplate them: "They seemed glad to get out themselves, and as if unwilling to be brought in." He was quite content in his house in the woods, where he lived for two years: "As I sit at my window this summer afternoon, hawks are circling about my clearing . . . a fishhawk dimples the glassy surface of the pond and brings up a fish; a mink steals out of the marsh before my door and seizes a frog by the shore." There was a train that passed nearby, and he called it "the iron horse." In several sections of the book, he defines his thought and himself as well: "I was self-appointed inspector . . . if not of highways, then of forest paths . . . trying to hear what was in the wind . . . I too had woven a kind of basket of a delicate texture, but I had not made it worth any one's while to buy them." This was because he believed that trade damaged everything it touched, and the case was the same with the potatoes and beans he planted; it's unknown whether he tried to sell them and it came to nothing, but he says: "trade curses everything it handles." He also says it's best to keep one's clothing for a long time because it adapts to the body and conforms with the personality of its wearer, and he finds patches quite dignified. Of his neighbors, he says: "It would be easier for them to hobble to town with a broken leg than with a broken pantaloon . . . We know but few men, a great many coats and breeches." What's more, he is against civilized society because, he says, the birds have their houses and the natives had them too, but in the society of his own time only 50 percent of people had houses of their own and the very poor lived in worse conditions than any Indian.

He studied construction in order to build the house with his own hands, and he was so pleased once he'd made it that he read the scraps of paper lying on the ground and said: "They afforded me as much entertainment, in fact answered the same purpose as the *Iliad*." He quotes a Hindu proverb, "An abode without birds is like a meat without seasoning," and adds: "Such was not my abode, for I found myself suddenly neighbor to the birds; not by having imprisoned one, but having caged myself near them." However, he met with an inconvenience: "One inconvenience I sometimes experienced in so small a house, the difficulty of getting to a sufficient distance from my guest when we began to utter the big thoughts in big words." When he built a fire in his hearth, he set a poem to it: "Go thou my incense upward from this hearth, / And ask the gods to pardon this clear flame."

He ate in the woods, played the flute, and skated on the lake, using a set of skates he'd fashioned himself. He watched hawks: "They are as leaves are raised by the wind to float in the heavens, their perfect air-inflated wings answering to the elemental unfledged pinions of the sea." He calls the owl: "Winged brother of the cat." He had squirrels living nearby, a hare that hid all winter under his cabin, and he listened to the croaking of frogs: "Each in his turn repeats the same down to the least distended, leakiest, and flabbiest paunched . . . vainly bellowing *troonk* from time to time, and pausing for a reply." He knew the order in which all the birds appeared and says: "Instead of calling on some scholar, I paid many a visit to particular trees."

DISCONCERTING STATEMENTS

Thoreau says that if a man were to build his own house, poetic thoughts would come to him, just as a bird sings while building its nest. Another strange thought is that it isn't men who are the keepers of herds but herds that keep the man, and they indeed occupy much more space than men. (He kept no herd, given all that about trade and because one should eat such animals as came his way.) He says:

"I like sometimes to take rank hold on life and spend my day more as the animals do . . . As I came home through the woods . . . I caught a glimpse of a woodchuck stealing across my path, and felt a strange thrill of savage delight, and was strongly tempted to seize and devour him raw; not that I was hungry then, except for that wildness which he represented. Once or twice . . . I found myself ranging the woods, like a half-starved hound, with a strange abandonment, seeking some kind of venison which I might devour."

And he later expresses something I heard two ornithologists in the present say as well: that the hunter may be the greatest friend of the animals he hunts. He adds that young people should be educated to become hunters, for then they would have much more knowledge about their prey than the poets and philosophers, who view them from afar. Thoreau generally refrained from eating meat and was of the opinion that people would cease to consume it in the future, "as surely as the savage tribes have left off eating each other." Although he adds: "Yet, for my part, I was never unusually squeamish; I could sometimes eat a fried rat with a good relish, if it were necessary." But he feels guilty when he longs for tea or coffee, as if these were vices; he says that it's best to drink water; he recommends celibacy, to which end the best thing to do is to work without rest, even if it's washing stables. He never married nor was ever known to have a sweetheart.

RELATIONSHIP WITH ANIMALS

Thoreau befriended a mouse, who would come up to him and eat crumbs, running up over his boots and clothes, and he even fed it cheese from his hand. He discovered how a number of animals will hide themselves and remain motionless, as when the woodland partridge feels threatened and conducts her young from a distance, clucking away, while the young lie concealed in the grass. He says: "You only need sit still long enough in some attractive spot in the woods that all its inhabitants may exhibit themselves to you by turns."

He observes warfare among ants and says the only thing missing would be for them to sing their respective national anthems to boost morale within their camps, and when he saw some sort of winged cat with a thick tail, he thought it was a flying squirrel. He says: "This would have been the right kind of cat for me to keep, if I had kept any; for why should not a poet's cat be winged as well as his horse?"

As for wasps, he doesn't kick them out of his house, considering it flattering that they've found the place to be a worthy shelter. Some moles made a nest in his cellar and ate a few of his potatoes, and they made up a bed for themselves with brown paper because "even the wildest animals love comfort and warmth as well as man." In spring he saw the animals leaving their burrows. He had neighbors in the woods; he also went into town with some frequency and would show up in a lecture hall with a sack of corn or rye over his shoulder. Sometimes while in town he would seek out shortcuts so as to go unnoticed. I'd have liked to see what some neighbor from the town or out in the woods might have written about him.

PYGMY OWL

The Creatures of Azul

WE'RE IN the living room of a chalet in Azul. Florangel (the owner), Ana (her daughter), Carlos (Florangel's brother), two payada performers, and Osvaldo Urbina, who clarifies: "I'm a troubadour, it's too much to say payador." Later on comes the poet Roberto Glorioso.

I got off the bus and headed straight for the payada performance. I went from the solitary seat, where I'd sat and looked out to see many cows and snowy egrets, to this living room so bustling with visitors and talk. The conversation about various creatures was so intense they were conjuring up the words to testify to the intelligence and clairvoyance of animals. And it seems some people have such great enthusiasm for this improvised song that there was once a veterinarian in Azul, so they say, who sent a colleague his diagnosis of an animal in ten-line stanzas. The same man said that children should be taught from a young age to think in verse, until one morning they wake up able to talk that way. People also told of how he took to religion in the last days of his life and would give his confession . . . in verse.

The art of payada is very old and supposedly came over from Spain. Payadas are sort of like duels over knowledge, wit, and cunning, all expressed in verse, and in former times they did indeed end in a gaucho duel. The verses from a payada made in Azul in 1934 attest to it: "The payada songs were over / and would finish in a duel." (At that point, the words were recorded in shorthand.)

Wisdom is often related to animals. In one payada, which took place long ago, they're riffing about tinamou eggs. One payador passes the challenge to another, asking him for the color of the bird's egg, and this one responds:

> *The eggs of the martineta*
> *do you know why they are green?*
> *well I'll tell it to you straight*
> *although it pains me some to say*
> *for the bird will feed on nothing*
> *but the purest wild insects.*

Later on in the same payada, one shoots back at the other:

This boy repeats more proverbs
than a parrot in the summer heat
and he's more eloquent even
than a statesman from La Rioja

It's interesting to think that in times past the payada was a fight to the death. Giorgio Colli, the Italian philosopher, maintains the same thesis regarding the earliest Greek wisdom, that it was based on how the oracle's meaning was deciphered: a verbal fight arose between two sages, and the one who lost had to die. But let's go back to the payada in the living room. The first to sing is the horse trainer Tata Gallo, age twenty, who wears a beret that covers his head completely with room to spare; he's skinny and serious, not breaking a smile once even though the people were heaping endless praise on him. He's immune to praise, looking at the others with his grave eyes and continuing on his way. In his song, he cuts to the chase, making no flourishes or detours. He's singing of a wounded palomino horse. Florangel, who's sitting next to me, says:

"There are loads of witch doctors around here who cure children and calves with indigestion."

Hugo, the payador professor, responds to Tata Gallo with further prolegomena:

I'm going to sing in just one breath
for I want now to invite you
to spill us out a song about
the creatures of this land

And then he poses a question, which is a challenge:

The rhea, if it's so wise a bird,
why does it never sing?

At Florangel's house they run a payada workshop; it's egalitarian, and professionals, wranglers, and humble country folk all attend. She tells me: "There was one lawyer who just couldn't pick up on the rhythm at all, though he had his heart set on it." I missed the response because I never carry a recorder, but swear I was very interested:

I didn't catch the answer
for I carry no recorder
I won't try and make a hash of it
I don't want to get it wrong.

The payada continues at a strong tempo, and Professor Hugo, at another point in the same line, says:

A very fine response indeed
your country proposition
but now I'll open up the gate
to keep this winning streak
I'll sing of the viscacha.

I don't know how, but they go from viscachas to horses in two seconds. Tata Gallo sings of the scrap merchant's horse, bringing home the bread, and then the weasel, terror of the henhouse, and then the ferret, "quite an understated creature." Someone suggests that they move on to the *cifra* song form, and they begin singing about the present:

And now if my guitar does pray
that from the heart I sing
we'll pop open the wine
and raise a toast to tradition.

And Carlos, Florangel's brother (whom she once set a cow loose on in the watering hole), recites:

I'll go along as best I can
and tell you, payador,

> *that to open this wine bottle*
> *a lovely thing for sure*
> *I'll need a bottle opener.*

The professor then recites a poem exalting the loyalty of horses; it's about a man who was left behind by all his children, but his horse stayed with him. Then another poem, dedicated to the colt: "He bares his teeth when shown the strap and saves his yearling dignity." At some given moment, as if they've made it through the register of animals, they begin taking shots at each other as though in a private duel, paying no heed to the others, pushing a bit at each other and then pulling back. Tata Gallo, who looks like Baby Jesus there among the doctors of this payada religion, calls the professor "old man" in verse but then backpedals and calls him "master." And it seems to me that the art lies in this act of advancing and pulling back so the thing doesn't break out into a gaucho duel, as in times past.

. . . . . .

The next day we're in the very same room at Florangel's. She, her brother Carlos, and Urbina, there to speak more in private about animals. I'd been hoping to interview Carlos, who knows a great deal about the subject, but in that house, so crowded with people, three amount to one somewhere else. I ask: There's a saying that refers to people who enter houses without asking for permission, "he comes in on his own, just like a sparrow." Which animals will enter houses?

Carlos: Mockingbirds get in to steal crumbs. They're very sociable. Pigs come in too, they'll look you right in the eyes, also lambs, calves. Horses come in looking for sugar.

Flor: My daughter-in-law, Romina, had a pig that she'd take right next to her in the car, nicely bathed and settled in.

Carlos: I had a very intelligent horse that used to come in and eat the dogs' kibble, but when it didn't find any, it went through the house looking and got spooked and confused and knocked all my stuff over. I also had a pig who acted as godmother to the cows.

Me: How do birds give each other warnings?

Carlos: The owl sends out a warning for all, then the lapwing repeats the call, much more stridently; they have a system of repetition and warn of abnormalities, for example a man crossing the land on foot. The southern screamer is a nocturnal messenger.

Me: And what about the relationships between different animals?

Carlos: Ewes are terrified of dogs because they can't recover from their bites, so they'll use cows for protection since they do try to defend themselves. Cows are scared of dogs because they can eat their babies; cows are very curious and also scared of the unknown, it might be a single color, something moving. They get scared when they see blood, or if they see a creature getting the whip, they turn tail.

Me: And what can you tell me about the conjunction of quadrupeds and birds?

Carlos: Birds do a bit more than just picking off the bugs; it's protection, vigilance. Lapwings, owls, and southern screamers are all lookouts. Another interesting thing is how they take turns: some sheep eat the tall grass, then others come to eat at ground level, always in the same order. Cows take turns drinking water, there's always one who drinks first and then another who's always second, and if one doesn't respect the turns, they'll butt into her.

Urbina: They always butt at chest level.

Carlos: Polled cows (the ones without horns) defer to the ones with horns.

Me: And friendships between animals?

Urbina: My dog lets the cat nurse at her breast.

Carlos: I put out feed with a pitchfork, and there are horses who are buddies with the cows; the cows have friends among themselves, the horses too, and they always walk around close together, indifferent to the others.

Me: What about animal memory?

Carlos: A horse won't want to go to a place where some harm came to it; I think they know how to tell each other tales and don't only do utilitarian things.

Urbina: I had a bag dog, a biter, and when he'd come find me to play I'd put on some leather gloves; when I gave some indication that I didn't want to play, he'd bring me the gloves to put on.

Me: And do they perceive the deaths of other animals?

Urbina: Horses don't, but cows hold a kind of vigil. They all get into a circle surrounding the dead animal and make a distinctive lowing sound.

Carlos: One horse neighed to me twice before he died.

Urbina (serious): He was saying goodbye.

Carlos: Horses have something like five distinct neighs, one for calling to a foal, one when they're spooked, one for challenging another to fight.

Urbina: They raise a challenge by sticking out their chests. Another neigh is a groan of impotence and rage when they're being broken, another is for when they've been left tied up too long and are thirsty.

Carlos: I think all creatures spend their lives observing us.

Urbina: You start plowing, and up come the chimangos, and the gulls, to get a look at what you're doing.

After that we went on with a series of philosophical-scientific asides, problems that they and I raised in turn. For example, how can it be that, with monkeys and humans being practically the same species, there's so much variety in size between gorillas and the little monkeys that fit right into your hand. There aren't any men that can fit inside your hand. They noted that people in Japan had managed some very tiny horses, but we quickly moved on from those mind-boggling enigmas.

Me: What are flocks of sheep frightened of?

Carlos: The unknown. For example, if I put a donkey inside their corral, one that's a stranger to them, it sets off a scandal.

Urbina: Bulls tend to be aggressive. When they see that people fear them, they get emboldened. Cows fight just like the bulls, head on.

Me: To wrap this up, Urbina, can you tell me which animals are found here in Azul?

Urbina: Mules, armadillos, rheas, tinamous, guinea pigs, ferrets, otters, viscachas, foxes, weasels; the giant armadillos (nearly extinct) are the biggest.

Then I went to an outdoor patio, where a very large toad was awaiting me: it had been years since I'd seen one. I made some comment, and they told me that toads are very intelligent, but as I didn't want the toad to be intelligent, I said goodbye, and Urbina, the troubadour, drove me to my hotel.

The Birds

Konrad Lorenz, a specialist in birds, wrote a book: *Er redet mit dem Vieh, den Vögeln und den Fischen*, "He Speaks to the Beasts, the Birds, and the Fishes." Hardly a flashy title, but it's a reference to the powers once attributed to King Solomon. Lorenz lived in a house where he kept a raven, a rat, and a few crows, among other animals. The rat would bite off pieces of the sheets to make her nest more comfortable. He also had a parrot who would say good morning, good afternoon, and good night at the proper hours. One day, the parrot became quite agitated, and he squawked: "The chimney sweep came." He'd heard him mentioned only once, but to a parrot, the man must have been like a bird of prey, that is, danger from above. This parrot once went missing for a while, and when he turned up again, he provided a clue as to what had happened. He squawked: "Caught in a trap, caught in a trap."

Stephen Hart describes a parrot practicing the words he's learning on his own at night. What do birds say when they chirp? According to Lorenz, it's localization: "Here I am, here I am." And also when a place is good: "It's nice over here." According to Hart, they communicate territorial defense as well, something along the lines of "Keep out." A single species can have seven or eight distinct melodies, and they also learn the dialects of their neighbors close by. Hart says that one species of hen, the bantam, which has many predators, has completely different communicative clucks for danger from above (flying birds) and danger from below (weasels). Lorenz says that birds who've lived in captivity with human beings don't know which species they belong to. They fall in love with human beings and may attempt courtship, unfurling their plumage at them. And not just humans; I read somewhere that a peacock once tried to seduce a nearby turtle. One wonders why a peacock would do this, but after all, looking at human examples, the bird's behavior answers to his intense drive to strut his stuff, to peacock, and after all, as the pre-Socratic Greeks said that Eros bleated like a ram, howled like a wolf, and bellowed like a bull. Beneath these various guises, in reality, lay Eros.

In his lovely little book *Historias de Pájaros*, Javier Villafañe presents the habits of these birds and the names they're given around Chile, Bolivia, Peru, and Brazil. For example, the southern screamer, a kind of giant lapwing with wing spurs, is called *tajac* by the Toba people, while ovenbirds are known as *caseritos* in Argentina and Uruguay. If an intruder gets into its nest, an ovenbird will mortar up the exit with mud, suffocating it inside. (I've read somewhere else that ovenbirds will bring in fireflies to light up their nests; birds enjoy shiny objects and bright colors.) Seriemas will follow people dressed in bright colors, yellow, red, orange, and they're also little thieves, making off with scissors, spoons, and thimbles.

The hummingbird is called *beija-flor* in Brazil and *kori kenti* in Peru and Bolivia. Hummingbirds sleep in midair and make their nests from cobwebs, as spider silk is sticky; they can set one down on any point they choose and it will stay fixed. The great kiskadee is called *cacuy* in Argentina and *ay mamá yayá* in Peru. The shiny cowbird, in Brazil, is *maría-preta*.

The largest birds in Latin America are the rheas, and while running they unfurl their wings like sails to make use of the wind; the males do a deranged sort of dance to win over the females, performing for several of them. A rhea egg discovered far from the nest is called a *huevo guacho*. Thus the *criollo* expression, *Anda como huevo guacho*, "Going around like an orphaned egg" (single, without a partner). In the south of the country, these birds go by *choique*, and in the north, *surí*.

Juan José Arreola views ostriches as poorly dressed creatures (parts of their bodies are bald) and says of them that they are "shabby, sensuous, and arrogant." Arreola tends to view animals as if they were people in costume. Or rather as if they were only there to carry out a theatrical role for our benefit. He says of king vultures that they have "something upon their wings like ermine in an azure field, and a head of chiseled gold, adorned with precious stones." Of course, they have such colorful birds up there, while ours on the plains come in gray, brown—muted colors. An ornithologist from Uruguay once told me this is because the ones on the plains need to camouflage themselves or else they'd make very easy targets, whereas the ones in the jungle or the woods have to show up, make themselves noticed.

Owls have a reputation for witchcraft. They hypnotize their victims. However, the epithet for Athena, the Greek goddess, is "the owl-eyed one." That is, someone with penetrating and intelligent eyes.

Birds can weave, sew, and decorate their nests. Tailorbirds in India use spider silk for their weaving, and they can tie a knot at one end of a thread to prevent it from slipping loose. They make holes in the leaves of trees and pass the thread right through. They also build private little dance floors for use during their mating rituals. One bird species in Australia, having no colored feathers to collect, gathers together colorful objects inside the forest, and this dance floor simultaneously acts as a display window. The ornithologist Gerald Durrell says: "The satin bower-bird is one of the few birds that uses a tool, for he will sometimes paint the twigs used in the construction of his bower with highly coloured berries and moist charcoal, using a piece of some fibrous material as a brush."

One detail that draws everyone's attention is the range of a bird's flight. Some of them can go from the Arctic to southern Patagonia, and the real question is how they manage to arrive in the same place every year without fail. Temple Grandin, a biologist and ethologist who is autistic and works to oversee the treatment of livestock raised for consumption in the United States, says that autistic people can understand animals better than normal people because they think in pictures, the way some animals do; birds are able to arrive at and recognize places they have visited before because their brains work like GPS." She points out two very interesting things. First, that bird intelligence has only been studied for a relatively short time while that of monkeys is already taken for granted, and second, that researchers work with animals in captivity, which are therefore free from predators. She poses the example of a bird in the wild that faces eight different predators and so has distinct calls for each form of danger. She believes that animal intelligence is born of necessity. I'm quite interested in animal intelligence. She says that an African gray parrot has the intelligence of a four-year-old child; one of them is learning colors and shapes and receives a nut when he gets the right answer. Once, he guessed several colors correctly but the reward didn't come. Then the parrot spelled it out: N-U-T. No doubt he made a variation in order to elicit a result, as if to say, "I'm getting tired of this now." Another time, when placed before a mirror, he asked the ethologist about his own color.

But let's return to Lorenz, a character just as eccentric as the animals that lived inside his house. A goose slept in a bedroom every night, going out by day to stroll around the place, and a few cockatoos, a monkey, and several ravens used to enter the bedrooms, for which reason he placed his own baby in a stroller inside a cage. He describes how birds could fall in love with people; a peacock once fell for the woman who came to clean, and a rook once fell for him. But birds can't tell the sex of humans (though monkeys can). The rook treated him as if he were a female and would bring food up to every orifice in his face; he'd close his mouth, not wishing to eat that paste of worms, and the bird would stick it in his ear instead.

Another bird used to chase after him even if he was riding his bicycle. And once, after few of his birds had escaped, he got up on the roof of his house and hoisted a large flag, in black and yellow, using it to call for them. Below him, the whole neighborhood crowded in to watch.

And after all that, for two days, he incubated a clutch of eggs himself.

WHITE MONJITA

Onelli's Experiments and Observations

CLEMENTE ONELLI was director of the City of Buenos Aires Zoological Gardens from 1904–1924. A renowned naturalist in his day, he accompanied Perito Moreno on several of his expeditions to Patagonia. He came from the era when zoo directors would spend a great deal of time at their institutions, many long hours, and so he knew the animals' habits like the back of his hand. But Onelli didn't limit his observations to what he was able to see; as he describes in his beautiful book *Idiosincrasias de los pensionistas del Jardín Zoológico*, he also mixed different species in with each other to watch how they might interact. For example, he once released a snake inside the corral that housed the seriema and a few rails. Seriemas and snakes are enemies; the two stared each other down and stood on edge, face to face, and then one valiant rail jabbed at the snake's head with her beak, stunning it; Onelli later killed the snake himself, but afterward the seriema swung the corpse around a few times, dashing it against the ground. The Greeks did the same thing in the *Iliad*; Homer describes how they flung the corpses of their enemies about so as to denigrate them and, I believe, to verify that they were entirely good and dead.

There was another seriema Onelli never knew where to keep because she'd always slip out through the screen of the outside door if he set her loose, and she'd never accept any other companions in her corral, so he put her in with a few deer. They started trampling her, and she, weighing in at only three kilos, took them head on and began pecking at their muzzles; they, who all told weighed close to five hundred kilos. There was a period of a certain respect, but then the seriema, a fighter, confronted one deer; this time she was left quite badly wounded and with a limp. Once she revived, after some time, she gave her aggressor a peck and flew far away.

Onelli says that, during heat, it's common for birds, and all animals in fact, to become unfriendly and irascible; if a calf and a zebu are placed inside the same corral, they'll fight, and a gnu will knock over his mate. But, just as with humans, there were a few couples that never got along. The jackal, having been left a widower, was given an Argentine fox as his new companion, and he didn't take the slightest notice of her; he'd only walk around while she was asleep, and vice versa. A bear couple behaves the same way. While the male is out in the sun, the female will hide away to take her nap. If she eats at seven, he'll wait until nine to feed.

One night in January, at the hottest point of summer, Onelli threw two blocks of ice into the bears' cage to see what they might do: the female dragged her piece into a corner and sat on top of it; the male crushed it up against his chest, then he set up the pieces like a pillow and looked as if he were kissing them.

All of the animals could recognize the zookeepers by their caps, and if a man wearing a hat with a brim approached, they'd be indifferent. But there was one seagull who flew free in the garden and was fed by different zookeepers, and she'd follow anyone wearing a cap, hoping to be fed.

There was a little Bengal tiger, a cub that weighed only five kilos, and they set her loose to walk around the garden paths. Only humans would confuse her for a kitten; the animals were all well aware that this was something other than a cat. When they saw her going by, the monkeys would look on with curiosity, the magpies would emit little cries, the southern screamer too would set off a cry of alarm and fly far away, and in general all of the birds would become alarmed.

There was a heron that ran free around the paths and used to hang out on the terrace at the café so that people would give her treats, but she'd only eat certain kinds of pastry and would also chase after women in skirts. And if Onelli didn't accompany her to the café, she'd go looking for him, and if he offered her a dry piece of cake, she wouldn't accept it.

I'm interested in the ways in which animals sleep. Sometimes I wonder: pigs, do they sleep lying down? The zoo director says that nap time is quite important for the majority of animals; it's indispensable for lions, although, as they're very lazy, they sleep almost the whole day through. But at nightfall they make great maneuvers before bed, much like the twilight runs domestic cats go on, as I've witnessed in some households: and when the zoo visitors leave and the light fades, the guanacos prance, the zebus bellow and butt, and the fallow deer run. Sometime later, all are asleep, save for the barn owls and true owls who live by night, but they remain still, silent and unmoving. It seems some birds will go on chirping in muted tones even in their sleep. (On TV, I saw a sleeping hummingbird giving forth a soft sound: the reporter said he was snoring.)

Onelli used to personally tuck his favorite monkey, Jacoba, into bed, and he writes: "While I'm meticulously arranging her blankets so that she won't suffer cold, at the very moment when she senses I'm about to leave her, she immediately pulls the covers over her head, shrinking in on herself completely. If I lift the blanket, I find her there with eyes opened inordinately wide, and then I pull the covers from over her head and smoke a cigarette by her side, and only then will she go to sleep."

One Corner

O N THE CORNER where Córdoba meets Humboldt, all is dark and dismal. I'm headed toward Palermo Viejo; it might be a Soho, or some such place, with designer houses, immaculate cafés, and brand-new hotels. I cross the street to take a look into a shop—if that name applies—which is filled with indiscernible things. Lying stretched out, two dogs with a diligent but unwashed look. The shop, or whatever it is, stands out for its darkness within that already dark zone; the stone of its walls, black. The proprietor, in a dirty T-shirt worn with pride, is surrounded by old things jumbled together in no particular order. On the wall hangs a blackboard, like the kind made for children, on which I can make out a sentence written in chalk: "When you must choose among several paths, listen to your heart, it's never wrong." There are a few Chaplin film posters, one from *The Kid*, and beside it a map of Argentina. Old magazines piled high and even older clothing in boxes, although *boxes* is only a manner of speaking. The owner, who once washed and dressed might have the cut of a gentleman, tells me: "I'm not selling anything. This is my house, and I sleep back in here on a bed I found."

I decline entering his bedroom so as not to invade his privacy, but it forebodes a darker and more disjointed world than the one outside. He says:

"I don't buy anything; I get everything from the street."

(There's no need for him to say as much; I could already tell.)

"So, you followed your heart's command."

"Ah, no, I change that sign every day. Yesterday I put up: 'When teaching is an art, learning is a pleasure.'"

"Very good. I see some sheet music over there. What kind of music do you like?"

"Rock. Why are you taking notes?"

I explain. There's a brazier, and above it a sign: "Brazier." As if it is an object worthy of a name, something of value.

"I wear whatever clothing I can find. The women's and children's things I give away."

"And the dogs, what about them?"

"They sleep in here with me, but sometimes they don't let me go to sleep, they're so affectionate."

The dogs are highly entertaining, sniffing at every living thing that walks by, more than sniffing, examining. Could this be a distribution center with clothing for the poor and homeless, with magazines from out in the country, here in the middle of this void? I gaze at the magazines, which look like scorched papers, and at the life maxims. Such rarified aphorisms, placed in the midst of this display of what might remain at the end of civilization, seem as if they've come straight out of a disaster film. Only the smoke and little bonfires are missing.

"And how long have you been here?"

"Three years. I used to live in La Paternal, in a house, but it was very boring there, always the same."

A neighbor walks past; he has the look of a trendy city dweller, smartly dressed, his hair cropped short, and he says to this corner guard:

"*Chau, amigo.*"

He doesn't seem the least bit surprised.

"*Qué tal, qué tal.*"

The dogs, meanwhile, have a fine job, following every passerby and then returning to home base. And, as dogs can sense when a visitor is about to leave, they post themselves amicably at my side to say goodbye.

TINAMOU

Monkey Business

A POLISH PLAYWRIGHT, MAREK Kochan, wrote a play called *Macaques of Celebes*. He came to Buenos Aires to give a few talks on his theater and gave me a copy of the work. It dramatizes a resonant case, that of the monkey who took a photographer's camera and snapped some photos by himself. The photographer published and made money off these photos; activists from PETA brought a lawsuit against him. A court in San Francisco determined that animals cannot own copyrights. Although posed in other terms, the debate goes back a long way. Plato, who had an elevated idea of man's rank among other living beings, said that the head was of a more perfect form than the body because it was round, a round form being the most perfect as it recalled the perfection of the celestial spheres; on top of that, it was on the upper part of the body, and man was thus able to look upward. (Plato found the body rather ungainly with regard to form; he didn't find it particularly convincing.) He also claimed that man is the only being without feathers to walk on two feet. This was why Diogenes once demonstrated a plucked chicken and said: "Here is Plato's man." We may recall that Diogenes had no needs; he did his business close to the barrel in which he lived. Right there, more or less. He spurned the city and its ranks: the city, originator of philosophy. If Diogenes' line of thought had triumphed, perhaps those monkeys would be getting paid for their copyright.

It seems that monkeys follow the habits of the most prestigious members of their groups and seek out the same objects they use, imitating the behaviors and fixations of their cohorts of high status. For example, some Japanese macaques who live in a very cold climate discovered the hot springs, and now they bathe in them. But all of them? No, only the hierarchs. A crowd of plebeian monkeys is left outside, not permitted to enter, looking on with supplicant eyes at those warm waters with a privileged few inside. It's their lot to remain out in the elements, in the snow. Some thirty years ago, one monkey inaugurated the custom of bathing, even lathering up and all, and several others copied him, surely members of the high class. No doubt fashion and prestige have their exponents here.

On one TV program, I saw the following: Mari, an orangutan, chose her companion through photos, selecting him out of all the ones they showed her. She chose Pongo. At first he played hard to get, but later they became close companions and he'd always sit beside her, cleaning her eyes. And on another program, I saw a monkey courting her love interest like this: she'd throw a few heavyish stones toward him, then run away and hide. This went on for a couple days; he played it cool at first, but, after about four stone throws, he came around.

Capuchin monkeys, though they don't have the intelligence of chimpanzees, can use a stone to crack open chestnuts and go fishing in a stream.

Onelli says that monkeys can get chilblains (and when they have sores, it brings them closer together). And though they may have fought in summer, they'll come together in winter to keep warm.

Frans de Waal, the great Dutch primatologist, has studied chimpanzees and bonobos, which are close relatives of ours, but he says they've only been treated as members of the same family for thirty years, as it was previously thought they belonged to different branches. He describes one occasion when, at a viewing of a film about bonobos, a renowned ethologist (not an ignorant man), on seeing how the males submitted to the females (theirs is a matriarchal society), indignantly exclaimed:

"But what's wrong with those males?"

Interesting. Evidently one can't understand things that one doesn't want to happen.

All monkeys outside of captivity give each other warnings, using distinct screeches to indicate predators from above, from below, and many other things. I conduct a test with a variety of people and ask them:

"Did you know that monkeys studied by humans can learn to speak?"

A look of disbelief.

"It's true, using sign language, since they don't have organs for phonation."

Some of them say: "Ah, using sign language!"

As if to say, "So, they can't really speak," and then they calm down.

A Naturalist

I ASK FRANCISCO WHETHER he's an ornithologist, and he
tells me: "No, I'm a naturalist." I comment on the latest
philosophical and legal theories about animals, which grant them
certain rights; the language has changed as well, and, relative to
animals, we no longer say "man" but "the human," as though we
were saying "the human animal." He nods and adds, regarding his
position within ornithology:

"As scholars of birds and animals, we are generally divided into
two camps, the conservationists and the protectionists. I'm a con-
servationist; we don't get hung up over the well-being of individuals within a species but are inclined toward species conservation.
In the case of pests, for example the beavers that destroy other
species, we don't hesitate about killing them. A protectionist won't
kill a beaver even if it's a pest that's destroying the environment.

In general, though not always, protectionism is related to vegetarianism and veganism."

And I set about my haphazard questioning: "Why is it that birds from the plains and the meseta (rheas, pigeons, etc.) come in gray and muted colors while those of the jungle are generally colorful and have large crests?"

"It's because they have opposite needs. On the plains they have to blend in with the grass or the clay, otherwise they'd be highly visible to predators. In the jungle they need to exhibit themselves for courtship; the trees keep them hidden. In the jungle it's the most colorful creatures and the strongest singers who are the most successful because the animals will pick the strongest, the most colorful, the healthiest to be their mate."

"How do birds choose their mates?"

"Some choose by color, others by song, others by flight."

I mention two things I'd seen on TV that had struck me. First, an older bird had greater chances for conquest because he'd had more time to collect ornaments, which he used for decorating the dance floor beside his nest. He'd decorate it with cicada wings, fallen parrot feathers, bits of coal, etc. The younger one loses because he hasn't had enough time to accumulate very many goods. The second striking thing I saw was a little bird entering her suitor's nest, checking to see if it was stable, and if she didn't like it, saying: "I want a two-bedroom with a garage, *pobretón*." The female bird flies off.

"Do birds communicate among themselves and with other species?"

"Among themselves, birds communicate using songs for contact and courtship. For contact: adults with their chicks when they're out feeding, and with other individuals in the group for any sort of danger, such as predators, earthquakes, storms. Sparrows have dialects and will sing differently according to region; the dialect is taught to the chicks. Lapwings give warnings to other species, ovenbirds too, and many people out in the country view lapwings like guard dogs. As for other species, flycatchers eat in mid-flight and act as lookouts, and if a flycatcher leaves or makes an escape, the monjita will follow suit."

"What defense mechanisms do birds have in relation to predators?"

"Adult birds (pigeons, lapwings) will pretend to be injured so they'll be pursued instead of their chicks. And if a snake climbs up to the nest, the parents go after it and try to peck it down. When a pygmy owl perches on the branch, they all try to scare it off. They also have particular characteristics according to species;

there are some overfamiliar birds that will enter houses, like mockingbirds, great kiskadees, gulls; herons are unfriendly. To observe them I make a little noise and they'll approach. Swallows are almost never on ground level; they'll only come down to look for material for their nests."

"An ornithologist from Lima told me about crows' intelligence. Crows will occupy the nests of other birds and force them to raise their chicks."

"The corvid we have around here is the plush-crested jay, and she does little mathematical calculations and uses a tool to dig around. I saw a video of one bird catching fish by dropping bait for them. Plus they have great memories, always nesting in the same place every year."

"I've read that parrots suffer from stress and will pull out their feathers. Is that true?"

"Many birds suffer from stress due to fear of predators, sudden changes in weather, etc. When we capture and band them, they can get snagged or banged up against the bars of the cage. Birds have delicate hearts, and almost all birds in captivity have a tendency to pull out their feathers."

"I've read that some birds are attracted to bold and bright colors and will even follow people dressed in clothes that have them."

"Not all birds are attracted to bright colors. There's one bird in Australia that constructs a bridal chamber using a blue color. I've seen birds in Africa that decorate all in yellow, and others all in blue."

"And how is it that they can fly so far and reach the same place every year. How do they know the route?"

"In the Delta, a hummingbird turned up that had flown there from Southern Brazil. Hummingbirds can fly three thousand kilometers; they lose weight during flight. Biologists know when the birds are about to migrate because they set about eating nonstop for a long time beforehand. As for how they keep their bearings, there are several theories: one is that they follow the constellations, another is that they follow the earth's magnetic field."

I've noticed that ornithologists are people of few words and can tell Francisco is getting tired, so I'll bring the interview to an end.

"Why do people say, 'All talk, like the southern screamer?'"

"The southern screamer is a troublemaker, all bark and no bite."

"There are two sayings that seem contradictory to me: 'Play the partridge' and 'Don't flush the partridge.'"

"No, 'Play the partridge' means to conceal yourself, to blend in, because a partridge is the same color as its surroundings, and

'Flush the partridge' means to snitch, because they give themselves away with their wings."

"And 'More bowlegged than a parrot on foot?'"

"Parrots are no great walkers; they move oddly because of the shape of their toes."

And I held off on "Thin as an eagle's whistle" and "Suspicious as a one-eyed rooster." Suddenly Francisco's face lit up, and he went out onto the balcony with his cell phone and binoculars. There were birds in flight. He said: "That one's a falcon," and "There goes a hawk," and then "Look, look!"

He went on looking a while longer, and it made me feel jealous since I don't know how to tell them apart in flight. By the time someone tells me to look, the bird has already flown.

GUIRA CUCKOO

A Book for Thought

TWICE I'VE READ the book *Animals in Translation* by Temple Grandin—the reeducated autistic biologist and ethologist—and Catherine Johnson, and I still found striking novelties the second time I read it. The subtitle is *Using the Mysteries of Autism to Decode Animal Behavior*. Grandin is exceptionally gifted. Her work in the United States is to monitor the treatment of livestock, for both "humanitarian" and pragmatic reasons, so that people can eat the meat of animals without undue stress. She was given this oversight position because of her condition. For her, the entire process of mental deliberation happens in images, and the final judgement that emerges from these images, in concepts. For example, when observing a chute that cattle don't want to pass through, she will notice a detail the builders and operators haven't considered, such as something painted yellow that hadn't been there before. She knows what frightens the animals because she perceives the details, unlike ordinary people, who perceive globally, that is, by translating whatever is there into an idea. Autistic children have often been compared to little wild animals due to the vehemence of their expressions, but this is because they react much more forcefully to visual, auditory, and tactile stimuli. It's as if they're able to perceive the world in all its heavy materiality: they may end up feeling an embrace as a crushing hold. One woman with autism told the author that she couldn't stand the noise of the sea. Many autistic people need years of reeducation before they can face a visit to the dentist or allow someone to cut their hair. Grandin is able, in this way, to understand animals' fears, but the affinities do not end there; another similarity she registers between autistic people and animals is that, in contrast to ordinary people, they don't have affective ambivalence: they love or they hate. The only ambivalence cattle have is between fear and curiosity, and these reinforce each other; a cow must go up and look at something in order to know whether she should be afraid of it. Regarding animals' fears, she says their keepers know a great deal more about what's going on with them than the people who study them. She says that many things can frighten them, for example pieces of paper flying in the air or an article of clothing hanging up that isn't usually there or shadows on the ground. They can also get spooked by moving abruptly from a brightly lit place to an area of shadow, and she believes it's possible that they perceive contrasts of light and shadow as contrasts of depth (precipices).

And the more easily frightened an animal is, the more curious it is: it needs to know. There was a horse who was afraid of people wearing black hats (not ones of any other color). Tracing through his history, Grandin and Johnson learned he'd been abused by a rider who wore a black hat. They can also be scared by an umbrella opening suddenly before their eyes, or the blades of a fan when they're turning slowly, or a person on foot if they've only ever seen him on horseback. In short, it's the same fear of the unknown that all of us share, along with the tools to fit the incident into a known pattern. It seems that people with autism experience more fear of the unknown than others.

CAUSE AND EFFECT

Arthur Schopenhauer has already said it: "Understanding itself is direct knowledge of cause and effect." Immanuel Kant included the concept of causality within the categories or instruments through which we think. David Hume studied the concept of causality deeply, considering it to be a simple relation of antecedent and consequent; as something occurred in the past, so it will in the future, and in this way our knowledge is based upon simple beliefs. Johnson establishes great similarities between humans and animals with respect to causal thinking. In one section of the book, "Animal Superstitions," she describes pigs stomping their feet on the ground before receiving food because they believed it was this action that brought about the delivery of food; this surely came about because their stomping their feet happened to have coincided with the food delivery. It's the same behavior when a child puts on a little red bracelet before taking a test because she'd had it on while taking another test that went well.

MEMORY AND INTELLIGENCE

This "photographic" animal intelligence allows us to understand how, for example, a crow can bury some thirty thousand pine nuts over an expanse of several kilometers and later find them or how squirrels too can find the things they've buried, and it might also explain—although most ornithologists confess they only have hypotheses about it—how birds can take flights traversing vast distances without losing their course. A hummingbird can fly from Southern Brazil to Buenos Aires.

But she also makes very astute observations regarding the work done with animals in labs: an animal in a lab doesn't do things that are motivated by its own impulses or needs, but rather the things it's directed to do. It seems prairie dogs, which live in the United States, have a greater number of alarm signals than monkeys do with respect to predators, precisely because their foes are many and varied: they employ distinct alarm calls for humans, hawks, coyotes, and dogs, and they can communicate to one another whether or not a man is carrying a shotgun. Crows too can perceive whether a man is carrying a shotgun. Crows have the ability to use a piece of wire and twist it around in order to pierce into something, even though wire is not an element of nature. Monkeys, when they learn to speak using sign language, are capable of talking about objects that aren't present.

Alex is the name of one African gray parrot who's been trained by ornithologists to learn shapes and colors. He has the same level of understanding as a child at age four or five. He calls a shape "five corners." One interesting thing about this parrot's training: they didn't train him directly, as is typical, but worked in tandem with another person, as though training her instead, so that the parrot could see, because that's how they learn in nature, by watching others. What's more, as motivation, they showed him appetizing fruits in various colors, making the animal see there was something to compete for between him and the other person present.

And one thing happened spontaneously, since no one had taught him to spell nor to ask questions: after one session of learning colors, he planted himself right in front of the mirror and asked, "What color?" (He might as well have said, "Me, what color am I?") And the ornithologist told him: "Gray."

As parrots and parakeets are rather neurotic, surely the female, seeing the male pull out his feathers or do something indicating stress, would tell him to calm down, and he, seeing her circling round the house in unease, would say: "Take it easy."

The author makes an astonishing hypothesis, saying that all trained animals are made to respond to instructions, but if they'd instead been trained to ask questions, other results would have been achieved.

A few other fascinating topics come up in this book, for example animals who kill others without need; monkeys will kill other monkeys for pleasure alone, and dolphins will play with porpoises and then kill them afterward. But, to contradict the hackneyed observation that "man is more bestial than the animal because he kills without need," I believe it's the other way around: both monkeys and dolphins are very intelligent animals, and they kill because they're approaching humanity. There's something extra in their ideation process, and they kill as though committing a free act. But one other subject intrigued me, though I had no idea as to its explanation. Predators go after the weakest prey, but how do they distinguish which one this is? And, connected to that, how can a domestic cat sense that his owner is already inside the building before she comes up to the apartment? And another: "A herd of antelope won't show the tiniest concern about a pride of lions sunning themselves not too far away." How does she explain it? She says that they're experts in body language, and that a lion exhibiting the behavior of drinking water does not exhibit the behavior of stalking. A man with a shotgun has a particular way of standing. And a cat that recognizes his owner can pick her out by voice from several floors up if she talks to someone in the elevator, or if he sees her from the balcony, he can distinguish her from the other people based on the bearing of her body as she walks.

The author's most daring hypothesis is that human language began as musical, tonal language. She says that the tones of Mandarin Chinese have reminiscences of music, and there's a bird that sings in refrains, and she adds: "Maybe animals use tone to convey complex emotions to one another."

When I was in Bogotá, I went out for dinner with a writer from Curaçao to see firsthand how he spoke. I'd heard he ended his sentences with a click of the tongue, and I wanted to witness that marvel for myself. He did indeed end certain phrases by striking his tongue against his palate, it was like a resounding gong.

What touched me the most was her assertion that all mammals, or most of them, have friends. Even giraffes. I never would have thought it.

A Rural City

W HEN A FLYING dandelion seed or a lizard finds its way onto my balcony, I start to think about how this ground, all taken over by city, was once inhabited by mastodons and giant armadillos. Long after that, it was inhabited by pumas, wild boar, ostriches, and, in the rivers near the city, caimans. Before the Spanish came with their dogs, there were already some here, and the native people once made boots from their hide. With the arrival of the Spanish (more dogs), these became feral; the dogs would kill the horses and eat only part. They'd approach "the city," to call it that name, and eat the sheep kept there, just like that. There are many news stories from around 1730 about those dogs, which hid out in viscacha caves.

I've just read *Buenos Aires desde setenta años atrás* by José Antonio Wilde. It's part of a collection with a curious name: "Autobiographies, Memoirs, and Forgotten books." It's a shame this book hasn't been reissued, because the author provides a past account of Buenos Aires from 1820 onward. Transportation, customs, pastimes, ways of speaking; he gives us a very rough idea of what old Buenos Aires was like: a kind of quagmire when it rained, through which circulated a vast quantity of wagons, oxen, horses, and dogs. Other creatures too. He says: "At the siesta hour, there's no one to see on the streets of Buenos Aires but dogs and doctors." Beggars went about on horseback, to the surprise of foreigners, who'd only ever seen gentlemen on horseback. Milkmen and doctors rode on horseback as well. Mansilla describes how kids would steal the doctor's horse as a prank when he left it tied to a post, and they'd take it for a turn around the neighborhood, which, if there'd been rain, would be flooded over. And, perhaps owing to still-fresh memories of the outrages those dogs had committed during the previous century, the prisoners from jail would club them to death in plain sight of everyone. "Fortunately, that custom no longer exists," Wilde says; nor does that of giving a public horsewhipping to lawbreakers. He tells of how a tiger, having come up the river through the camalote grass, ate a priest's horse in a stretch of fallow land. A procession was once interrupted by two oxen making their way through the people; the saints fell to the ground, the people fled in terror, and the ones who'd come there together got separated.

This animal presence even made it into the theater, which was a kind of precarious shed where they performed plays that seem to have been meant for a peasant audience: an actor would imitate a rooster's crow, slapping his thigh. Until the year 1846, troops of wagons came from the inland provinces bringing wine, dried fruits, and alfajor cookies. The line of wagons stretched from Recoleta to Retiro. The ground was filled with marshes, the terror of the wagon drivers. Indigenous people would come to Plaza Once to sell ostrich feathers for making feather dusters as well as objects fashioned from cowhide, buckskin, fox and skunk skin.

Beef was cut up using axes. The most rebellious mules had their heads tied up with cloth, and when they rested, all of the ground was taken up by idling mules. The mules disrupted people's passage through the streets.

The most frequent journey made on horseback was from Florida to Retiro. (They used to say "El Retiro," "El Azul," "El Pergamino.") And even the most privileged families would travel to San Isidro by wagon, for there were no good roads, and going from downtown to San Isidro took about seven hours.

And so I don't find it strange, with such a past, that we have so many sayings involving cows, horses, and oxen.

CHIMANGO CARACARA

Ramiro Rodríguez

RAMIRO RODRÍGUEZ was a caretaker for wild animals at the former Buenos Aires Zoo, in the field of conservation (of endangered native species), and has since become a researcher with a focus on the rehabilitation of birds of prey. I asked him a few questions:

We've known about the intelligence of monkeys for a long time. Why did it take so long to discover that of birds?

In my view, the intelligence of monkeys and the genetic and morphological kinship that we share with them (especially with simians) led us, from the beginning of our studies into animals, even from the perspective of pet ownership, to conduct an endless number of assessments and investigations. The fact that they're able to communicate with us using words and ideas, and that they're the only beings apart from humans capable of doing so, led human beings to study them and spend a great deal of time with them. On top of that, they're charismatic and extraordinarily human in their actions. It's a mistake to anthropomorphize animals' actions, but from the beginning, educational documentaries, just like films and TV, took advantage of these nearly human characteristics, sometimes with the wrong message, to bring the cohort of monkeys and apes into the homes of people who had no access to see them in their own environments, in order to raise awareness.

I've heard several theories about bird migration, long flights spanning from the Arctic to Antarctica. Have you heard anything about how they orient themselves during flight, whether they take rests, etc.?

Bird migration is a subject I'm particularly interested in at the moment. In my training as a scientific bird bander in Europe, it was necessary to know all of their molting stages, migrations, and signs of age and sex for all the species present, and nearly all of them are migratory. There are short, medium, and long range migrants and they come in all sizes from a tiny passerine weighing in at eleven grams to an imperial eagle at five kilos. All of them, no matter their size, will migrate great distances under certain circumstances, from Northern Europe to Southern Africa or Asia, the same as they do in the Americas, from Canada to Patagonia. Their strategies for carrying out these journeys vary depending on each species. There are some, like swallows and swifts, that practically never pause along their journey, sleeping and feeding in midair. Other species have different sites for rest and replenishment. As a result of systematic banding, we know that individuals born in a place will return, year after year, to that same site, their birthplace. We also know the number of consecutive years a pair will return to the same breeding site; in the case of swallows, the same barn, the same nest. Many birds migrate in groups with the same species, others in groups with different species, and others alone. The V-shaped flight formations we can see from the earth are used to conserve energy; the individuals forming the point keep trading places to provide lower air resistance for the others. Flying in groups also brings them greater safety with regard to predators. How they orient themselves remains a mystery. There are the most varied theories and hypotheses. It is believed that the earth's magnetic fields aid in their orientation. Visual memory is also of great assistance.

Birds communicate among themselves and with other species. What information do they give each other?

Communication between birds is very rich and differs from species to species. A single species may have an endless communication repertoire, though it generally serves for communicating danger, mating calls, disputes, or to see which male is the most eligible, to demarcate territories, among other things. Many species, especially in jungles, give warnings of danger when facing the presence of a predator because they have the best vision, and other (non-bird) species use these danger alerts to escape in time.

You have established the intelligence of deer, something that is now being studied.

I'm not up to date on the studies being conducted at present. My work with deer was limited to their rehabilitation and care in captivity. But yes, I can confirm that they have high levels of intelligence. If raised from a young age, they can acquire the imprint of a human being and end up seeming like domestic animals: they can identify their "human mother" from among other humans, for example. This imprinting tends to be dangerous in the care of deer in captivity because the male specimens, once psychologically liberated from human beings, begin to view them as equals/competitors and end up wanting to compete with them over territory and/or females; the aggression may be greater or lesser depending on species, but in general they are all dangerous to deal with.

Experiments have been done with gray parrots from India, and it's now said that parrots generally do not speak in such a mechanical way as had been believed. Do you have any news about that fact?

Yes, the *yaco*, or African gray parrot (*Psittacus erithacus*), is a parrot species that inhabits the jungles of equatorial Africa. They are considered the most intelligent birds. Their intelligence is comparable to that of a four- or five-year-old child. I currently have the good fortune to be working with three specimens from this species, and it's incredible to see them using words and sounds for special situations. These are the parrots most often used in studies on intelligence. I can't remember the number, but they can learn and recall a vast quantity of words as well as when it's appropriate to use them. They also have great visual memory and can solve mental/mechanical problems without any difficulty.

A bird will notice if it loses its mate or its chick. How do they react?

Attributing human reactions to animals is a mistake; when a bird loses its mate or chick, after a period of readaptation to the situation, it will do what genetics tells it to do and look for another mate or conceive a new chick to continue the propagation of the species. Male falcons in the genus *Falco*, such as peregrine falcons, will allow other females of the species to enter and stay within their territory. There are studies confirming that, when faced with the death of the reproductive female, the male will select one of these females, generally young, in order to continue propagating themselves as a species. All birds, or at least the majority, engage in something called "replacement laying." If for whatever reason they lose their eggs or their chicks, they automatically begin a so-called "replacement laying." In a short time they are ready to produce a new clutch once more. In fact, this ability is used by breeders of many species to procure more clutches from a single female. The eggs from the first brood are incubated artificially and raised by hand or by a surrogate mother, and the second brood is raised by the original parents. This technique is especially common in the breeding of raptors.

Birds' courtship rituals are very flashy. In captivity, do they also set up dance floors and decorate them with little objects? Or how do they do it?

Those displays are especially common in birds-of-paradise, a family of rainforest birds. Studies have found that the better a male is at dancing and the better he is at building and decorating his nest, the higher his rate of reproduction will be. A male who is an excellent dancer and builder/decorator will have more chances to bring forth progeny, and his offspring will no doubt inherit the same abilities. The most capable one is also the one who will have the most children, and thus the species will grow stronger.

It appears that birds can fall in love with human beings who are close to them. Have you ever seen something like that?

That's called imprinting. It does happen with birds that are raised around humans from the beginning of their lives. It was initially confirmed and studied by Konrad Lorenz with his geese. More than infatuation, they view us as their equals, and so they want to fight or reproduce with us. It's most common to witness this in parrots, but it can happen with almost all species. It's a problem, because birds raised by or as humans rarely view members of their own species as equals and end up having difficulty reproducing.

The majority of predatory animals choose prey that is weak or unwell. How are they able to recognize that?

An animal that is sick, weak, pregnant, or young is at a disadvantage compared to their equals. And so they become prey. A predator, when selecting its prey from among a group, carefully chooses the smallest, the slowest, the least attentive, the most dejected, etc. Wild animals, to the detriment of the work of wildlife veterinarians, will give no signals of discomfort until very the last moment so as to prevent their predators from noticing their condition. When a wild animal shows any sign of discomfort, it is surely in its final moments and will most likely end up as another's prey. The circle of life.

Varieties

MONKEYS COME IN all sizes, shapes, and colors. In Boa Vista, Brazil, lives the bearded capuchin, who hunts by day, eats palm nuts, and will leave a nut on the ground to let it dry out, coming back a week later to crack it open with a large stone.

The aye-aye looks like a cross between a bat and a mouse, yet it is a primate.

Baboons in Kenya hunt flamingos, getting right into the water to catch them; howler monkeys have almost human mouths. In the Amazon lives the pygmy marmoset, which weighs about the same as a mandarin orange and can climb up to the canopy of the forest. The tarsier monkey is four hundred times smaller than an orangutan. Gibbons are acrobats and look around themselves as though they were humans. There are some tiny lemurs as well (these are primates), the smallest being the mouse lemur. It looks like a mouse with the face of an angry turtle. And long ago there were lemurs the size of gorillas. Then there are ring-tailed lemurs, with eyes like glass marbles; they leap with great bounds and sit close to humans with absolute confidence. Don't they have any predators? Why such familiarity? A ring-tailed lemur will sit right next to a man, legs spread wide, like an old man airing out his crotch. They all hold their tails upraised, and one will stare at a man with extreme attention.

Monkeys and lemurs can live in cold climates, or hot ones; they adapt to everything. Japanese macaques live at twenty degrees below zero, all covered in snow, but they have two layers of fur. In Madagascar, in a hot climate, there are white lemurs that can spring nine meters from branch to branch.

In Gabon there are mandrills with striped faces, and they come in many colors. They have straight eyebrows, which give them a wise and stern look; the most colorful male is the one who gets the most females. There are white monkeys, black ones, orange ones.

In India, rhesus macaques live close to the markets and work in teams. Instead of climbing along the vines of the jungle, they go across power lines. They enter houses, pulling open freezers and plundering them.

A baboon troop in South Africa has no trees to climb; they live in a flat terrain, filled with predators. At night they climb up into a cave using a rope left there by bat researchers. They keep their bearings perfectly within the darkness of the cave.

Capuchin monkeys, the ones with that modern hairdo, can fashion tools; they smash nuts using hard objects, and there are white-faced capuchins who will make themselves taller by placing one head on top of other (one positions himself behind the other so that he seems to have two faces), and in this way they appear larger and more imposing when confronting their enemies.

Orangutans know how to tie shoelaces, and they'll use sticks when they need to cross a river. The sticks are for calculating the depth of the water. And they're experts at escaping from cages.

Among the chimpanzees, there exists the figure of the one who sets the limits. I've seen the following: two females were facing their young, who were play fighting; as the fight was beginning to get out of hand, the mothers kept monitoring each other and their young, and, at some given moment, one mother went to wake up the matriarch, raising an arm to point out the fight between the little monkeys; the matriarch growled menacingly and the little monkeys settled down.

WHISTLING HERON

The Avian City

Miguel Santillán is only an amateur ornithologist, yet he has published more than thirty scientific works on the diets and parasites of birds of prey, among other subjects. He works as coordinator for the zoology department at the Museo de Historia Natural de La Pampa in Santa Rosa. And he is driving me out to the country, along with the owner of the bookshop Fahrenheit and his young daughter Delfina, to witness an avian world. We all sit silently in the car, hearing about the relationship that connects this Miguel to the other Miguel who lives in the country. City Miguel says:

"My conversations with Miguel deal exclusively with birds or animals. One night he called me around eleven o'clock and said: 'Miguel, it's the falcon, one of her feathers fell out.' 'Ah well, these things happen,' I said."

The two have already published a joint work on the procreation of the whistling heron. The whistling heron resembles other herons but with the addition of an absurd crest.

We're on the way out of Santa Rosa and the desert begins; there isn't a soul to be seen, only the posts of wire fences. Miguel says:

"Here's one."

As soon as he alerts us to them, birds take flight, as if they're only willing to show themselves in front of experts. But now I'm looking at the whistling heron in a guidebook, a gift given to me by a woman named Silvina, may God grant her many years. I'll have to keep this guidebook hidden so no one steals it from me. I look at the whistling heron: that rebellious crest gives it a lunatic air. Miguel says he's going to publish another paper with his country namesake, as the other Miguel made the first record of offspring. The two Miguels' avian streak runs so deep that, when I asked this one how long he'd known the other, he said:

"About six years now. But Miguel measures the time of the relationship by the falcon's laying cycle. He says: 'The falcon has laid five clutches since we met.'"

This observation lent me wings to ask one of those questions I ask. I feel they're a bit ridiculous or eccentric. I once read in the work of the Dutch primatologist Frans de Waal that birds feel the pain of others; when the gander's mate sees him fighting with another, her heart begins to pound. The question didn't seem odd to Miguel, and he gave me the impression that one could ask an ornithologist anything, that nothing avian is alien to them. Then he said:

"My wife, Soledad, is a zoologist at CONICET, and we studied aplomado falcons together. A mountain cat looted the nest and killed the female along with the chicks, and the male was left alone, screeching, beside the nest."

The photo of the aplomado falcon that Soledad used in her work had been taken by country Miguel, the one we're on our way to see now. I ask driver Miguel if birds have memories, and he says:

"In order to study a bird, you have to weigh it, measure it, band it—in short, you cause it discomfort. When the falcons see my car, they beat at the windshield."

The white monjita, the heron, and others appear, perched on fenceposts. Miguel says:

"Here come the peregrine falcon, the owl, the chimango caracara. The chimango is very intelligent."

"How so?"

"He can open a bag of trash with his beak. There was an experiment where they prepared some boxes for one, and he was able to open them. Cowbirds are brood parasites; they steal from the property of wrens or sparrows and make another animal care for their eggs. The cowbird follows the cow."

"Why's that?"

"It's the reason for the English name, 'cowbird'—the cows flush up insects as they walk, and the birds catch them." We're almost there now, thirty kilometers outside Santa Rosa, and we turn to the subject of birdsong. Miguel says:

"Mockingbirds imitate other birds' calls and sirens and any other noises they hear."

"I've read a little about stress among birds; I don't know why I found it more interesting in birds than in humans, but I read that, under stress, parrots will pull out their feathers."

"Yes, that's true. The cause of stress in birds may be hunger or proximity to a particularly feared predator."

Now I know why I find stress in birds interesting; it's more of a spectacle with them. I also learned that the lapwing warns the owl when there's danger. I found myself asking why this, why that, as if some response would reveal to me the mystery of life, and so I decided instead to ask Miguel about himself. He was from the Mendoza province, lived in Córdoba, had developed an interest in birds, and was now traveling from Santa Rosa to Puerto Deseado studying the brushland tinamou. I thought about how ornithologists are like birds: the birds travel to lay their eggs in other lands, and the ornithologists lay down a few eggs of their own in different places while following the routes of a species. I asked for his email: It's raptorchaser@ and so on.

. . . . . .

As we were coming to a stand of trees, we saw a group of six rheas running at full tilt. Behind the grove stood the house of Miguel Ángel Fiorucci, man of the country, lover of animals in general and birds in particular, and photographer. The house had indoor plumbing, a cozy living room, and two or three bedrooms, all done in masonry, but the facade had not been painted since 1947, when it was built. Miguel Ángel says: "I like everything to look natural." It seems a bit chipped and faded, but, after all, the house doesn't have to compete with any others nearby: the closest neighbor is three kilometers away. The same goes for Miguel Ángel's clothing; the birds aren't going to reproach him for having his sweatshirt on backward. He wears pants and a dun-colored work shirt as he bustles about with the nests and birds.

He receives us in the living room; his home is heated with firewood from caldén trees. There is a TV, and he explains: "I only watch the news and listen to Latin music." He speaks of his life with a peaceful expression and only gets worked up when talking about poachers and livestock rustlers. He says: "Several poachers have stolen the batteries I use to collect solar energy. And the rustlers, when they want to steal a sheep, they mimic its bleating. I used to go hunting when I was seven years old; I caught a siskin in a cage, I kept a sparrow tied on a leash—the first thing that draws you to animals is hunting them, keeping them, trapping them. Usually the kind of people who hunt end up being the ones who love birds. They hunt ravens around here, but it's been a very long time since I've gone hunting for anything."

I look at Miguel Fiorucci and see something of the bird about him, and something of Don Quixote de la Mancha as well. I've seen that gray-brown outfit before on other ornithologists, dressed as if to camouflage themselves, and I find it an outfit well-suited to the unrest of the times; in the seventies, there was the cultural worker's uniform, a denim jumpsuit.

On a low coffee table, he sets out some little alfajor cookies and invites us to have yerba mate. Suddenly, he brings the conversation to an end and appears carrying a platter, one half filled with ground meat and the other with eggs and a variety of fruits. Can the meat be for us, this early? No, the food is for the birds; he serves them this platter three times a day. He says: "They eat the finest quality lean ground beef. I spend seven hundred pesos a month on ground beef alone. Once a week I go to Santa Rosa, to La Anónima. My wife lives there; she comes here on the weekends. Ah, and if I don't have the cash for it, I pay with my wife's card. And they also eat grapes, which are very expensive since they're not in season."

Miguel walks ahead of us, platter in hand, and we all head toward a tree full of birds, who have surely spread the word among themselves by now: "Miguel is coming, it's feeding time." These birds hunt for their food in mid-flight. Gabriel the bookseller says:

"I've never seen anything like it."

The birds fly low as they pass, and Miguel explains:

"The chimangos feed first so that they don't take advantage of the others, then the guira cuckoos, the great kiskadees, and finally the brown cacholote and the green-barred woodpecker. A piculet makes a little hole and then a woodpecker will come along and enlarge it, so I put epoxy putty in the nest to stop them from taking over."

All this time, we've been accompanied on our excursion by two dogs and a kitten that's been trained not to kill the birds. The kitten and the dogs accompany us with such diligence as we observe the other animals that they look like tour guides promoting these corrals, nests, and dens. Still with them, we go over to the mill where the monk parakeet's nest used to be; the kestrel has taken it over, and Miguel attaches a wooden box because the nest is deteriorating.

We continue to a shed like the kind used to store tools, but he keeps twelve cats inside it to stop them from eating the birds.

"Sorry," he says. "This is a little messy."

More than messy, it is dark, an absolute darkness, so that I imagine this must have been the very place in the depths of the earth where Zeus cast Hephaestus with a kick that rendered him lame. Only two of the twelve cats appears, and they don't approach. Miguel saiys:

"They're unsociable. I feed them chicken giblets."

Then, still escorted by the dogs and the kitten, we witness some of his handiwork: a cage where he keeps the parakeet so the chimango can't catch it. He used a few branches to fashion a kind of lookout for the owl to perch on, and since the tree is dead, he mends it with thick paper and wire. He has a long stick topped off with a mirror that lets him look at birds' eggs that are very high up. He says:

"When Mamá was living up in the mountains, they used to eat songbirds' eggs."

Then we see a corral with a sheep and an orphaned fawn that he'd brought home. The sheep, drinking water from a tap, is called Cordera; city Miguel tells me that he used to keep boar piglets, and they'd come right into the kitchen and eat biscuits. The piglets had names: Javi and Violeta. He also appears to have had a calf and a boar that would sleep out with the dog.

I pet one of our accompanying dogs, and Miguel says:

"My dogs never even chase after hares, I don't let them. A lot of farmers grumble about birds, but I've only become more of a protectionist."

(I could already tell.)

What does a ruler need to govern a city? A knowledge of its inhabitants and those in the surrounding towns. He traveled to Bahía Blanca to study one species of owl. As for knowledge of the inhabitants of his own area, that's something he has in droves. (He knows what spooks the horse: when it sees a shadow, or when a rhea spreads its wings; the cow: unfamiliar people and sudden movements.) He provides shelter and food to all of the birds that come his way. He also fulfills a policing function: the birds eat following established priorities. I forgot to mention he's quite a good photographer as well; he has a striking image of two cara-caras, their wingtips raised, surrounding an armadillo, and the caracaras' attitude is one of fascination at what they are seeing.

And now, back in the car on the way into town, city Miguel tells us how his namesake avoids owl nests when he's out plant-ing. The other farmers usually just kill them. And he won't tell his brothers when a puma is prowling in the fields, since they're hunters. He also describes how, when some Italian growers came to see the way they worked the fields in La Pampa, Miguel didn't show the slightest bit of interest in the subject of increasing production, nor in demonstrating his own to them: he took them out to see the nests he'd crafted by hand, and the ewe with the fawn, and other things of the same order.

Animal Planet I

THERE'S A MONKEY from Manaus that has a sort of white woolen halo, and when they sit down the wool looks like a cushion or a pillow; I'd call them gust-of-wind monkeys, for the wind must rustle that coat of theirs. Seated, one might be a royal authority, yet his rascally eyes reveal a lack of awareness of his power. Surely that cushion must get snagged as they go from branch to branch in pursuit of a spider or an ant. The great egret has a long and hollow bill; it looks foolish with such a long thing, as if they'd forgotten the bird has to eat and gave it this prosthesis later on. I imagine the bill is always making a racket, clap-clapping all the time, stirring up the fish; that egret is quite skinny. The wren makes a good father, but he takes lovers, and he'll bring his mistress of the moment a gift of a little leaf, a little flower, yet for the lady he built the nest with, he brings nothing.

Frank, the Spaniard who visits creatures all over the planet, calls the tortoise "Auntie" and the caiman "María José." He calls the elephant "Uncle" as well. Informing the TV audience that elephants are afraid of mice, Frank tosses one to an elephant, but the animal doesn't get spooked; the locals present are dying with laughter to watch the scene, for they play the same game with their youngest children: they put a wind-up mouse in with the elephants, and that really does scare them. A woman from the group of natives stares at Frank and says: "Look how big he is, and still such a baby!" How diplomatic of her; everyone looks amused. Frank picks up a snake with a stick and says: "Up you go, *chavala*, I've got you, aren't you a beauty, but you've got a nasty temper . . ." Later, he finds an enormous crocodile in his path. It opens its mouth and has a throat so large and flat it looks like a city plaza. Frank says: "In a while, crocodile!" There's a turtle catching fish and insects; it has a kind of beak, and he says to it: "I've got you now." Some children are playing cricket in the background, and he inserts himself into the game: "I'll try to give the ball a good whack." But after that he goes along his way and sees a mongoose, which looks like an otter, and then a five-meter-long king cobra appears, and he says: "That's right, I can see you're a little riled, look at how she rears up, what a lovely thing, what lovely eyes you have."

Up next we see a torpedo frog. Frank's appearance is curious.

His clothing looks ragged, and his expression as well, as if he were a wild beast assailing the others, wishing for victory or death at one of their hands. (I think he had an accident.) To the torpedo frog he says: "Up yours, you just pissed on me . . ." Then a baby owl turns up, and "Your mother sent me to tell you to come inside." Then he goes back to where the native people are: he's there with a cobra and starts saying "cuchi-cuchi" to it. One of the locals gets up from his seat and says, sternly: "The cobra needs to rest."

There's another creature seeker, quite a bit older, who has a face that says "Please forgive me." If this human (that's the new terminology) were in an office, he'd be earning his place by dint of being patient, smiling, and playing the fool. He's likable; some animals give him the slip because he's feeling bloated: "I ate too much rice and eggs, I shouldn't have done it," he says. The guilt, the apologies. He goes in search of pandas, but there are few left in the forest, and he doesn't find a single one. (Sometimes they aren't able to find an animal and will distract the TV audience with whatever shows up along their way.) Of course he comes across something: it's a cross between an ox and a goat that stares at our explorer with a face that says "Who do you think you are?" This explorer, when he doesn't feel like showing an animal or isn't able to, will say: "I mustn't disturb him, he's sleeping."

He addresses the animal with respect, as though talking to a boss in the office. He finds the pandas in a scientific refuge where fifty Chinese researchers are measuring and weighing the animals, carrying them and their cubs to and fro. The cubs weigh one hundred grams at birth, and the fact that they go on to reach their adult weight is astonishing. Being so plump, the bears look as if they must reach their great size through a series of internal inflations, like something blew them up from within. While they are cubs, the pandas play at rolling around and look like furry balls (it's no odd thing that they're adored in China), and they grip onto the bamboo shoots with their little paws in a gesture of submission and harmony so that they seem to be praying.

In China there are also flying squirrels, which shoot from tree to tree.

While Frank could be called a kind of intrepid clown, there's also another explorer of a different species who's something like an overcautious boy scout. He points out all the dangers of the jungle, mixes in with the locals only when it's strictly necessary, and brings along porters whose movements and calm expressions contradict the dangers he proclaims. In Venezuela, he saw the giant centipede, a venomous species that will attack mammals. This centipede has not changed in three hundred million years. That detail amazes me. It reduces to dust the very existence of cities, of cultivated land, of private concerns and those associated with environmental pollution.

This same boy-scout investigator is going to Vietnam in search of the giant water bug that lives in the rice fields. On the way he encounters the albino cobra, which eats meat and "liquifies it like a milkshake." Later he says: "I'm enjoying the pleasure of a python breathing into my ear." When he leaves the snake behind, he gives her a kiss. He travels to the city to speak with a Vietnamese expert; at the market they sell dragons eggs larger than melons. They go to a restaurant where he's served fried scorpion, and he says: "I've spent so much time around scorpions, this feels a bit wrong."

They eat the giant water bug as well; it comes as juice served in a little cup.

PLOVER

The Lima Zoo

I'M MAKING MY WAY toward the Lima zoo, remembering all the zoological parks I've seen in my life: there's one in San José, Uruguay, where they have a monkey and swan enclosure. The monkey has a two-story hut on dry land, and surrounding this hut is a pond where the swans go around and around. The monkey lives in fear, like a paranoid homeowner, for the swans are cat burglars; almost without looking, quickly and with ease, they'll steal something they see in the grass that belongs to the monkey's garden. The monkey spends his time going from top to bottom, climbing upstairs to get a better view of his enemies and then down again, a tree branch in hand, hoping to give them a whack, but they've already made their escape.

At the Central Park Zoo in New York (air-conditioned), there is another concurrence of swans and monkeys. The latter are numerous and live on a kind of rocky island, while the swans move through the water surrounding the island. I watched the monkeys at their usual activities: some picking for fleas, others sleeping, one standing watch. Suddenly a swan went by, honking loudly, and all the monkeys, as if choreographed, completely switched their positions and roles. Something happened, something I can't explain. Nor can I explain why this concurrence of monkeys and swans is repeated.

I've been to the zoo in Asunción, where there's a sign in the snake room that says, "No Screaming," and the one in Mendoza, quite lovely and built right into the sheer mountain slope, uphill, so that if you make it up there you can see the whole city. Also the one in Frankfurt, where I saw an orangutan meticulously smoothing out his bed of grass before sitting down, the way you might straighten sheets. And I also went to the one in Santiago, Chile, although, since I had someone else with me, I can't remember which animals I saw. I like to visit zoological parks because I believe the animals and placards in them share national characteristics. The Uruguayan monkey, as would be the case for an Argentine monkey as well, must contend alone against injustice and abuse, while the ones in Central Park quickly line up in a distinct way as though obeying some mechanical and universal code of conduct. The monkey in Frankfurt, while smoothing out his bed, keeps in mind what ought to be, a central concept in philosophy.

At the Lima zoo, there's a fence of blue morning glories and crowds of high-school kids, brown; at first glance, from a distance, the animals look brown as well, in gray tones with bits of tan and black. The dusky hawk is inside a cage with a placard: "Don't come past the barrier, I don't want to hurt you." From time to time the hawk lets loose a foolish authoritarian cry, hopping his way around and screeching when he alights. Next door are the llamas, curious but discrete, and if you fix your attention on them they'll avert their eyes like city people who only look when you're not looking. (Cows and pigs will look you right in the eyes.)

Among the animals there is also the Pampas cat, striped and larger than a domestic one. It has a sign: "I'm on a diet, if you give me food it may be harmful to me." It's different from the signs at the Buenos Aires Zoo: "Do not throw food to the animals." These signs are a demonstration of Lima's diplomacy, deterring you with good manners. Nearby is the long-winged harrier, whose stare moves rhythmically from one corner to the other so as not to miss a single thing.

The condor has a white collar, and when he spreads his enormous wings, the children watching let out great shrieks. They're there with a teacher who looks like a woman to be reckoned with, and she asks them about things they already know: "Does he have feathers? How many feet?" The teacher has a voice like a street vendor, calling out, "They eat roadkill!" The kids already know this, as you can tell by their resounding and exasperated "Yes." I, who am taking notes, make it around twenty children who are doing the same. Nearby is the Andean puma, and he has some difficulty sitting down because he's getting old. In Colombia, they say of very hesitant people that they "have the three speeds of a donkey: idle, standing, and sitting down." Well then, the puma has three speeds for sitting down. Next to him is the oncilla, a miniature tiger, with a sign: "Noises bother me, please don't knock on the glass." Next door, the viscacha, who has ears resembling a rabbit's and moves her mouth the same way they do. People call them mountain rabbits. The hummingbird is called *korikenti* and the great kiskadee *Ay mamá, ay mamá yayá*. Next I saw the toucan, who has a Paraguayan hammock hanging in his space for when he rests; he was scratching at fleas. I went back to look at the condor, and later on I read about him: they can reach four meters in length with their wings extended, can fly at up to ten thousand meters, jet cruising altitude, and belong to the same family as falcons, caracaras, and vultures; they like to have a falcon for their neighbor. And the name 'condor' comes from Quechua, *kuntur*.

In the trees along the path that leads the way out of the zoo are the great kiskadees and the lovely fence of blue morning glories. As soon as you leave, the city appears with traffic lights, cars, and a few little bars. And this all belongs to such a different world that the zoo seems like a piece of the country wedged inside a vast city.

Clara's Parrot

C LARA HAS TOLD me so much about her parrot Perico that I finally go to see him. Something she'd said left an impression on me: if she's busy cooking and the telephone rings, the parrot will squawk: "Leonella, pick up!" (Leonella is Clara's daughter.)

And there we go, to a house on the way out of Ezeiza, home to not just one but two parrots. Marta the parrot is also there in the cage next to Perico's, silent and overshadowed next to her companion's antics. Each in a house of their own. Marta the parrot (I can't bring myself to call her Marta directly, the way they do) looks over at Perico as if he were some dastardly relative who gets caught up in a fresh scandal every day. She stares at me with great attention as well. I comment on this.

"Ah, she never misses a trick," says Clara's husband.

The house provides a great deal for the parrots to study; Clara and Alberto move about swiftly. While she cooks, Alberto sets the table. Clara takes it for granted that the parrots are able to understand nearly everything.

"Do you have a mirror?" I ask. She gives me a hand mirror, which, to the parrots, would be body length. I want to see if they'll look at themselves in it. Marta recoils into the back of the cage; she saw something, though I don't know what. Perico won't even look because he can't stop putting on his show: he laughs with a human laugh, a sinister and forceful cackle, and it's hard to believe that it could emanate from a body so small. I recall what Frans de Waal said about the tests humans put to animals; it's never certain to what extent they really are able to solve them because, like Perico, they have other concerns. He won't look because he's already watching himself. Clowns don't look at themselves in the mirror. Clara goes over to the cage and tells him: "Do the caveman."

Sure enough, he makes a full loop upward, skirting along the cage, and then another around the base. Then he laughs with that laughter of his meant for special effect. Beyond the half-closed door appear two dogs, one wearing a supplicant expression, wishing to enter. Perico looks at them and says: "Enough!"

Clara says that he doesn't like dogs much; he'll say, "Enough" and, "Go away, filthy dog." And he once said "Enough" when two girls, age five or six, were having a fight in the house. When Clara tells him to soak his cracker in the water because it's too hard, he goes over, dips it in, and makes himself a bit of soup.

Perico says "Clara" with a rasping voice. The voice disappoints me slightly, as if I'd been expecting him to speak like a presenter on the BBC. But it's time to say grace, and Clara says to him, emphatically: "Look at that long face!"

Perico inclines his head and covers his face with one foot, as though despondent.

Both of them tell me that if someone makes a strange noise with their body, Perico will say "Yuck"; he's done so just now, but I missed it and am not about to go asking them to make strange noises just so as to study him. Then Perico coughs, a measured cough, like he's faking it. Throughout this entire display, Marta the parrot has remained forgotten, and it's clear that she's used to being overlooked. She's all eyes.

"She doesn't speak?"

"No, only in private. She's shy."

"And what sorts of things frighten them?"

"They're scared of thunder and storms. Whenever he hears the sound, Perico will squawk, 'Inside.' And when the telephone or the buzzer rings, both of them squawk, 'Go.'"

I think that, just as other animals will signal each other if there's some need (due to danger), parrots speak properly in limit situations. Fear of a storm, for example, or deep emotion. Clara says:

"One time Tato came to visit; it had been a year since I'd seen him. Perico used to love him, and he recognized him and squawked out, 'Tato.'"

Then she adds: "He practices words at night—it's like he's running lines."

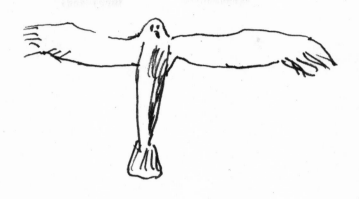

LONG-WINGED HARRIER

Naturalists in the Nineteenth Century

B IOLOGISTS USED TO BE called naturalists, and some of
them have led positively fascinating lives, like Alexan-
der von Humboldt, Aimé Bonpland, and Henry David Thoreau,
to name a few. Andrea Wulf talks about them in her book *The
Invention of Nature*. What stands out is the vigor of their travels,
what with the number of places they visited and the time devoted
to them. Humboldt and Bonpland departed Spain on a course
for Venezuela, and it took them forty-one days. (They traversed
practically all of South America in their search for plants and animals.) On the coasts of Venezuela, they captured a monkey that
amazed them: he was able to distinguish, from among the images
in the zoology books that Humboldt had brought with him, the
insects, his favorite food; he'd pick them out and stare at them.
By sea, the way from Cuba to Cartagena took them more than
two weeks, and from there they made for Quito. They crossed

the Andes on foot. In Colombia, they lost part of their collection of plants and insects, and their shoes were destroyed; they pressed on, barefoot. At every step they lost some more of their material, yet still they kept their spirits. They put in four and a half months going from Quito to Lima. They crossed Mexico and from there went on to the United States. Bonpland, in one ascent up a volcano, stood at the very edge of death but was saved. I imagine Bonpland wishing to give himself up and die in the path and Humboldt driving him on to climb just one step more, for Bonpland was the more sedentary, the sort of adventurer to take up settlement, while Humboldt loved perpetual motion. Nevertheless, the extreme effort of those journeys must be good for you; both lived for more than eighty-four years. What drove these naturalists to make journeys of such a dangerous kind, not just for them but for the material collected as well? (On one occasion, they sent two cargo loads to Europe separately for fear of their seizure on the high seas.) What was it that moved them? A disdain for city life. Humboldt thought of Berlin as "a little, illiterate, and over-spiteful town." Bonpland lived in Buenos Aires for two years and was extremely bored there. Thoreau was a poet, but he read Humboldt. He didn't like to travel, though he lived in the woods outside his own town. He would collect plants in his hat and later conduct investigations.

Near the border between Colombia and Venezuela, Humboldt loaded a stray dog, eight monkeys, seven parrots, a toucan, and a macaw with golden feathers into the boat. He called them his "traveling menagerie." But as he went along in the boat, he saw animals that he regretted not being able to capture. Humboldt says it was a shame the monkeys didn't open their mouths as the canoe passed them so that they "could count their teeth." Humboldt kept a pet chameleon. (How can it have been domesticated?)

Another thing that united Bonpland and Humboldt was a love for South America. Later, Humboldt goes on to Siberia but says the expedition was not as satisfying as the one he'd made in South America. For South America had what all adventurers desired. To be the first to traverse a territory; to discover new species of plants and animals. And also to sense that, in the jungle, there is always something beyond. The city creates limits and is limited; within the city the animals are fenced in, while in the forest lies a great concert where the monkeys screech, the birds sing. Already by that time, people had done away with the idea of nature as a fixed image, its species stable, to instead attend to the transformations of animals and the relationships between them. The jungle was not viewed as a static thing; Humboldt perceived it as a play among forces that complemented each other to constitute a dynamic whole. He says that the jaguars hunt the tapirs, and the hunt startles the monkeys, who set to screeching in turn, and their screeches wake the birds. Man feels close to and also a part of the animal kingdom. Johan Wolfgang von Goethe, who was a friend of Humboldt's and had read him, had a mannerism that used to alarm his neighbors: he'd fling his arms about in a conspicuous way, to make you notice their presence. Like they were wings; a way to prove that man and animal had common antecedents. He'd say: "That's how I walk more naturally." Yet it's not just a similarity in organs that establishes a connection between man and nature but the feelings the latter brings out in the human being. Humboldt says that "nature communicates in mysterious ways with our most private feelings." A poet like Thoreau is a naturalist as well, and he has the same intuition as Humboldt; it seems he used to imitate porcupines. The writer Nathaniel Hawthorne said of him: Thoreau "is an intolerable bore." I look carefully at Thoreau's portrait. His face is that of an angelic rustic; his presence would not be appropriate in an urbane salon.

Naturalism and Politics

Not only was there then a clear relationship between botanists, zoologists, and fiction writers, but they were linked to the politics of the era as well. Those investigative expeditions needed funding and therefore depended on the government of the day. But more than that, the very material they collected was viewed from "political" perspectives. George-Louis Leclerc, Comte de Buffon, without ever having seen America, claimed that the plants, animals, and people there were weaker than those in Europe, and that no large mammals or civilized people lived there. The president of the United States, Thomas Jefferson, stung by these observations, sent him word that even the weasel was larger in America than in Europe and dreamed of finding a living mastodon somewhere so as to put a lid on him. Buffon, who came before Humboldt, had, based on his statements, an irascible habit of judging. He said that the jungle was full of venomous insects and decaying plants, that the toucan's bill was a monstrosity, and that in America everything was mediocre. He never deprived himself of making value judgments.

. . . . . .

If there's one subject that has interested me for a long time, it's Bonpland's life; basically, he was a botanist, though a zoologist as well. Unlike Humboldt, who came from a rich family and was more accustomed to dealing with courtiers, Bonpland steered clear of contact with city folk. On his second journey to Latin America, he came to Buenos Aires because they'd offered to have him set up a zoo like the one in Paris, but the whole thing went up in smoke. His was not an organizational mind, if anything it was disorganized, and he didn't want to do too much documentation of the things he found. Humboldt would complain about him because he didn't want to write books on botany; even so, Europe was introduced to six thousand new species of plants thanks to him. He always wanted to return to America and while here had changed his name; he'd been Aimé but called himself Amadeo or Amado here. He was persecuted politically after the death of Joséphine, Napoleon's wife. Forced to flee from France, he found it a good opportunity to return to his beloved Latin America, and I suspect he also did it to flee from Humboldt, always apt to be scaling the high peaks of some place on the earth. He wasn't one for heights; any scrap of land with a bit of green suited him fine. When he reached the border of Paraguay, where he'd been planning to stay and conduct research, President Francia had him arrested under suspicion of espionage (Francia had his reasons to distrust both the English and the French, though he wasn't right in this case), and he was confined in the interior of Paraguay. They gave Bonpland a ranch, a cow, some tools to make a garden, and left him there to soak in a kind of limbo out in the country. There he could conduct his investigations in all freedom and tranquility; he seemed content. Meanwhile his European wife is left in Brazil, anxiously asking after him. Humboldt inquires as well, and even Bolívar grows interested in the fortune of Amado, who remains in the country, ignorant of these concerns. Bolívar writes to Francia, threatening to invade Paraguay if they don't release him, and even plans a rescue mission with Argentine soldiers, but it seems Simón Bolívar wasn't all that knowledgeable about how politics worked down there. Francia doesn't disturb Amado at all apart from confiscating his letters, something that doesn't seem to have troubled the naturalist very much. He starts a new family in Paraguay and remains there for eight or nine years. Over the course of those years the livestock multiplies; by the time Francia lets him go in a caravan of wagons, he leaves with something like a thousand head of cattle and all of his research. He's a man in good supply. He settles down in Corrientes and starts yet another family there. (No more is known about the first wife or the Paraguayan family.) In Corrientes and all around the country, the Bonplands are numerous; they're scattered all over Argentina. In the city of Corrientes, I met Marian Bonpland, Amado's great-great-granddaughter, a criolla girl with pale eyes that must have come from her ancestor, and in one of the Carnival parades she danced her grandfather's whole history. The people of Corrientes know Bonpland's story well and from time to time will put on a show about his life during Carnival.

Surroundings

G EORGE MUSTERS, in his book *At Home with the Pata-gonians*, says that the people there have a custom of allocating a few mares and stallions to a child at birth. The parents cannot sell or trade them; they're the child's property. If a boy dies, they'll also kill the dogs, horses, and other animals that accompanied him. It's the same when an adult dies; the animal he used to use is sacrificed and his clothing and belongings burned. And couples who have no children will adopt puppies and allot horses and other articles of value to them.

Margaret Mead, regarding the indigenous inhabitants of New Guinea, says that everyone there is constantly touching and hugging each other, and when there are no other human beings nearby, they'll embrace a dog or a pig; she says that they pamper pigs so much they seem like dogs; they'll bow their heads when reprimanded and nuzzle up against a person's body when they mean to ask for something. On the day of the festival of pigs, the people sprinkle them with holy water and will often sing the name of their favorite pig in refrain.

Perito Moreno tells of how once, when he asked an Indian friend, María, if he could borrow a horse from her, she said:

"Ask the dog."

She added that the dog was the owner of four horses, two cows, and a bull, and she also told him that her puppy once chased after a guanaco that had come up to the tents and came back from this pursuit bleeding, and in response to this the women all cried and sacrificed a mare to the Evil Spirit so as to ease the animal's suffering. Perito Moreno also describes how some guanacos once came up to him when their curiosity conquered their fear. He whistled *Rigoletto* for them, and he says that they "paid great attention, stretched out their necks, and made pirouettes, but I think they preferred *Aida*."

Returning to Musters, he says the spoiled puppies of the Indians ride on horseback along with the smallest children, and he once even saw a hen laying on horseback, brooding just as well as you please! And he adds that one of his native friends, old Orkeke, dispatched one of the Chileans who was passing through the camp to cross the river with his puppies up in his arms so they wouldn't get wet.

Musters also says the Indians tame horses more gently than whites, so that there are no nervous horses, and they'll put leather shoes on them for climbing up steep or rocky slopes.

In the indigenous children's world, animals are very present; skunks and rhea chicks serve as playthings, and the parents will make them miniature bolas to hunt for small animals. In his friend Orkeke's tent, there were two domesticated skunks who carried themselves like kittens.

To the indigenous people of Patagonia, animals are the equivalent of the mountain to the populations who live in forests or jungles: the mountain gives them everything. Among the Patagonians, animals provided everything: they ate the guanaco's meat and used their hide to make cloaks, blankets, and tent coverings; they fashioned pipes and used ostrich feathers to clean them. The shell of a rhea's egg served as a cup for coffee. The armadillo's shell was a vessel for drinking soup or storing sewing tools. From the guanaco's forelegs they made little boots for the children, and from the guanaco's tendons they made thread to stitch their blankets.

There were, in that region, migratory birds: blue and orange parrots that flew from Entre Ríos to Patagonia. The natives asked Musters where England was, and he said: "Where the sun comes up." And they would think, quite logically, that if there are traveling birds, there might be traveling people as well.

GREAT EGRET

Animal Planet II

A T ANY TIME of day, if you turn on the TV, you can find at least four channels devoted to animals: on one there's the dangerous "black widow," on another it's the life of the bottlenose whale, and farthest afield, the habitat of the cheetahs and all the poor creatures they eat for breakfast. Not to mention the dogs shooting hoops, jumping rope, or dancing tango. Whether they're wild or domestic, beautiful or loathsome as a lizard, their keepers call them "good girl" or "sweet boy." The North Americans will measure them, weigh them, and put them in cages to bring them to the jungle and so fulfill the destinies nature had set for them, just like in a movie I saw: it was about a couple who was keeping a lioness as a pet. (The woman was more in favor of the lioness; the man only just tolerated her, and so the lioness aimed a snap at him.) The pet slept at the foot of the bed. The woman decided it was time to return her to the jungle so she could lead her own life, but this had to be done gradually: the lioness needed to learn sex, and so they all went to the jungle in a van to make sure their pet would have a charming date. The woman said: "I feel the way I would right before a fifteen-year-old daughter's first date." The lion who approached didn't have the same idea: when they released the domestic lioness to face her destiny, she didn't know the rules of courtship; the male lion came up as though saying, "What do we have here?" Before beating an Olympic retreat, the lioness was hit with a swipe that left her dizzy. They quickly loaded her into the van, while her adoptive mother, to make sure she wouldn't feel embarrassed, told her: "You did great. Rome wasn't built in a day. We love you, you know we love you." The second encounter went even worse, because they approached a shorter-tempered lion and he almost killed her. But the man took out his shotgun and let loose four charges at the lion; he was plenty inclined to let off another two at that pet of his wife's, but he knew if he did she'd be capable of killing him with that same shotgun as soon as he let his guard down . . . Yet these North Americans are tenacious: in the end, the lioness found a boyfriend and left for the jungle; her adoptive mother cried. How can they be so tenacious and yet so sentimental at the same time? They won't back down before any creature, no matter how fearsome, but will try to train it. There's one program, *Animal Rescue*, where they collect animals who are sick, abused, or in need of retraining. It advertises itself like this: "Eels with attitude problems, goats with bad manners, monkeys with abandoned-child syndrome . . ." On that program I saw a hedgehog getting an operation: he lay on a large gurney, like a little ball amid the snow, and the surgeon said: "We'll have to put him on an IV for now." I never would have thought they'd give a hedgehog an IV.

But all kidding aside, some animals are fascinating. Monkeys have incredibly complex social organizations, with a troop leader and a successor awaiting his turn; they lick each other to signal submission or reconciliation, and they have friends and enemies like we do. Once I saw an anthropologist showing a male monkey an image of a female because he had to choose among several: the monkey threw away the image, a sign he wasn't pleased. They also move together and go to fairly distant lands to explore new territories, and if they see a cave made by an intruder monkey inside their own territory, they can tell the difference and will seek him out and subject him to eviction law. And the look some monkeys have, as though understanding something, yet at the same time pierced with the sorrow of not knowing . . . To paraphrase Friedrich Nietzsche, when he says that man made himself into an animal full of future promise, for me, the monkey seems to be an animal brimming with future promise. And they grow old, just like we do: they get white hairs, their mouths curve in a sign of skepticism, and their eyes turn more beady and penetrating, proof that this penetration, in us, is a sign of time and necessity, not of our having become wiser with age. *Salú*, monkey dearest.

The Anteater

THE ANTEATER looks like it was created in parts, like those houses with clashing add-ons. They're always walking hunched over in search of ants. According to Toba legend, when a great fire came and laid waste to everything, the people sought shelter inside a well; the deity allowed them to come out as long as they didn't look around, but the first to come out was a little old woman, hunched and with bent fingers, very curious. Since she disobeyed, she was turned into an anteater. (They're crooked, slow, and walk with their feet bent inward.) They defend their young from the jaguar's attack clumsily, in fits and starts, and people don't consume their meat. Why have they caught man's attention? For their looks. From bears they have only the fur, the snout comes from a tapir, and the claws look like the talons of some enormous bird. And people wonder why they have a mouth so small you couldn't even fit a finger inside and an extremely long tongue. In summer they shade themselves from the sun with their enormous tails (their only beautiful feature). And they can swim, crossing rivers just like that. They only live in America, and when the Europeans first saw them, they were astonished by their appearance. They also called them *caballos hormigueros*, ant horses. One will cover himself right up to the head with his tail, whether from rain or sun, and that blanketing tail makes him look more absurd than he is, but now I'd like one myself so I wouldn't need an umbrella or a hat to block the sun. In the mountains they can get by on ants; in captivity they have to be fed a supersmoothie of yogurt, eggs, mincemeat, vitamins, fruit, and low-lactose milk. On a TV program, a woman was keeping one as a pet. What would they name him? I'd call him Ruperto, but I wouldn't want him as a pet. He looks like an outlandish walking hut; it's unsettling to see a hut moving around. The woman who keeps him as a pet has a face that says she believes in destiny and will accept and celebrate any incident fate or chance may bring. She says, with a smile filled with understanding:

"He likes to get into the freezer."

Of course she lets him. Mysteries.

PLUMBEOUS RAIL

Sayings and Legends

L EGENDS EXPLAIN how beings and things came to be as they are. The questions posed in legends are not so different from the ones we ourselves wonder. Who invented the zipper? And the pillow? The difference lies in the response. Whether you believe in God or evolution, a visible form remains fixed until the contrary can be demonstrated. For now, if life did, as it is supposed, begin in the seas, then our arms were once fins. The only way legends differ from science is in their temporal perspective. Science needs to approximate how many million years it took for those fins to become arms, but legends do not; that's why they begin with "A long time ago . . ."

Among the Guajiro people in Colombia and Venezuela, this is the explanation for how cloth first came to the earth: a deity changed form in order to teach the humans how to weave. For them, animals were people who had once been punished for something they did; a god had caused them to talk in an unintelligible way, but before this punishment they could speak clearly. In Guajiro legend, visual transformations are accepted quite frequently. The group lives in the jungle, where everything rots and decays and many things undergo visual transformations. If scents and tastes can transform so much, why couldn't beings and objects transform? In fact, because these people go from the jungle to the coast, they call the octopus a "water marmoset." They pay attention to the fact that both move in a particular way, not to visual consistency.

Hummingbirds lives among us. The Inca called them *korikenti*, the Guaraní *mairumbí*; the Brazilians say *beija-flor*. They're the tiniest of birds and build their nests from spiderwebs and tiny little leaves. And one will sleep upon a leaf; there are many legends about them. One says they were begotten by a fly. Hummingbirds have roused affection in everyone, excepting the Mapuche people, who consider them evil birds, perhaps owing to their powers; they can fly from Southern Brazil to Buenos Aires Province and from New York to Yucatán, all with that tiny little body. No doubt the Mapuche would have thought "someone else was helping them to fly so far" (and ornithologists have several hypotheses regarding the long distances the birds achieve and their ability to recognize the route, but these are only hypotheses and some differ greatly from others).

For the anteater, I know two legends. They aren't creatures of an elegant aspect; they look like shacks on legs. One legend says they were created in a hurry, for in the beginning the gods created the jaguar, which is very attractive, and second they created the tapir, which is average as far as its looks go, but when they made it to the anteater, they forgot about the teeth. He asked: "So what am I going to eat?" "Ants," they told him. Another legend says that when they made it to the anteater, they were running low on material, and that's why they have such tiny mouths.

What would Juan José Arreola say about the anteater? That it's like when a mother serves up some horrible dish and says, "Well, it is what it is." The indigenous legends are more compassionate than Arreola; it would seem these people care a bit less about beauty or grace.

The Mocoví people from Santa Fe used to hang an *aguará guazú* (which looks like a large fox) from a tree and start mocking it collectively, owing to who knows what prior history. The Mocoví would hunt monkeys in the following way: the men would set about making boots in front of the monkeys, who were watching them from a tree. The boots were tiny, as though made for monkeys, and the monkeys would come down and want to try them on, but they'd have resin or some adhesive material inside so that the animals were immobilized and could be caught. This invention reveals their understanding of a desire in the monkeys similar to that of humans: if I like the boots, maybe they'll like them as well.

Ornithologists tend to have habits similar to those of the birds; they are migratory. Miguel Santillán, the ornithologist from Santa Rosa, once said to me: "I'm headed to Northern Chile now, to spy out some birds."

Alex the Parrot, and Others of That Ilk

NOT SUCH A LONG time ago, around 1980, it was discovered that some varieties of parrots are able to speak sensibly. I began to investigate parrots after María, my pedicurist, told me how she'd once forgotten her parrot out on the patio in the middle of a storm, back when she lived in the country. She forgot to cover him up, and parrots are terribly frightened by storms. They woke up in the night because the parrot was desperately shrieking: "Help!" In other words, finding himself in a tight spot, he said the appropriate thing. Charles Reinhardt, in his treatise on animal psychology, describes a parrot who learned his cagemate's name; the other died and three new companions were brought in, then another who resembled the one that had died. He called this one by the first companion's name. There's one species that's particularly intelligent, the African gray parrot. If they're served some food and then given a signal that they should wait because something better is coming, they'll hold out until given the thing that they like more. The Russians have studied African gray parrots and have taught one about incentives: he knows how to recognize a triangle and a square; he can say when two things are equal to one another or when they are different.

Alex is an African gray parrot, trained by his ethologist, Irene Pepperberg, in 1977. He can recognize a key and its color. He'll say: "Green key." And, for another object: "Blue wood." And when asked for its shape, he calls a pentagon "five corners." In other words, he understands material, shape, and color, and he knows how to add small quantities. Parrots can be rather hysterical, and more than once Pepperberg has had to say to him, "Calm down." Once, she entered the room in agitation, pacing back and forth several times, and the parrot squawked, "Calm down."

The crow has also been studied recently. It is now known that crows will modify branches to turn them into hooks, and not just branches but also pieces of metal they find lying around. It's believed that they can recognize the voice behind any cry emitted as well as its maker's status. The magpie, who belongs to the same corvid family, will look at herself in the mirror; if a mark is placed over her eyes, the bird will scratch it off. If a jay, who is related to the crow as well, doesn't want a competitor to steal her food, she'll pretend not to be interested in it. That is, they have the capacity to deceive and also to mock: she'll provoke a dog while she's far out of reach and play around with the ethologist, hiding things to make him look for them, and he does the same to her. Crows can learn to soak bread or crackers in water for the amount of time necessary to get them just right, in other words, not so hard that they're impossible to eat, nor so soft they disintegrate. One experimenter gave some nuts to his crows, cracking them open in front of them; the crows went off to their hiding spots, took out the nuts they were hiding there, and brought them back to the man.

CACHOLOTE

The Bird of a Thousand Songs

COLOMBIA PRODUCES surprising books, for instance this bilingual edition of *The Fantastic Aviary of Sir William McCrow*. The book includes some beautiful illustrations of birds and a map on that uses birds to indicate all the parts of the world where this McCrow has gone: Europe high and low, the United States, and Canada; in Latin America, Venezuela, Colombia, Brazil, Uruguay, and Southern Chile; he's been to Asia and Australia too. He traveled for fifty years in search of the Bird of a Thousand Songs, whose existence had been mentioned by an indigenous man from Guyana. What can such a strange book be? A treatise on ornithology? No, for it invents imaginary birds such as the golden mockingbird, which "can perfectly speak Russian, Arawak, French, Quechua and 396 other languages." Then there's the trumpet bird, which he discovers in New Orleans: "Today I have discovered a new bird who was perched on the head of a young black man named Louis Armstrong. This bird, which I have named the Trumpet Bird, has made his nest on this man's head."

Not all the birds are imaginary, because he does, for example, deal with a toucan he saw in Colombia, and he collects the observations of Comte de Buffon and Charles Darwin. Buffon called the toucan's bill monstrous, and Darwin wondered what such a large apparatus could be for. McCrow says: "Tucans use their long beak very much like painters use their palette of vivid and festive colours. It is where they combine, mix and prepare the most beautiful shades with which they paint the tropics." Throughout the fifty-year span of his travels, leaving Europe and coming back again, whenever he draws near to the continent he thinks of his colleagues in the ornithological society, believing they will condemn him and scorn him for his discoveries. Is this author crazy? Yes and no. Who would travel for fifty years in search of something he never finds? Yet has discovered over twenty new species of birds along the way. And why did he spend so much time away from Europe? Initially because of the death of his father, and later, as he says: "I wish to distance myself from the madness of the wars led by the ambitious British Empire and instead, lose myself in the songs of birds and find the Bird of a

Thousand Songs, even if it is the most inefficient labor ever initiated by a son of the British crown." In 1935 he goes to Germany and can sense the coming war, and he says: "I don't like this one bit." Is he really a Sir? No, the title was given to him by a member of the London ornithological society, mockingly, because of his vagrant appearance. Were his journeys in vain? No, because he did discover new species. Is this written seriously or in jest? In the text "Levitating Hummingbird," he tells of how he encountered a new species of that name. And he says: "My colleagues from the British Academy of Sciences have been mistaken in thinking that their quickly flapping wings cause their hearts to beat so rapidly. Now I am convinced that their hearts beat one thousand times per minute because of the love they feel for the birds of paradise." And didn't the pre-Socratic Greeks say, "Eros bleated like a lamb, bellowed like a bull, and cawed like a crow?"

The whole thing has a philosophical undertone: beyond visible appearances, there is a potent force that moves the world and the beings who live upon it: Eros. And couldn't the hummingbird's attraction toward the bird of paradise be called Eros?

In 1928, still looking for the Bird of a Thousand Songs (he's been searching for close to twenty-seven years by now), he returns to London, where he submits his work for the consideration of the Academy. They say: "The research (if it can be called this) carried out by Sir William McCrow lacks scientific foundation. It presents no proof of the existence of such 'mythical creatures' with the exception of a few poorly drawn illustrations. His notes resemble more closely to a proof of the insanity caused by one who is obsessed with finding a figment of his own imagination." McCrow transcribes the Academy's verdict in his book. But now why would the Academy call him "Sir" if it is a facetious nickname? And if he knows the Academy will reject his work, why does he submit it to them? And why would the Academy give a verdict for something like that? In 1934, he says: "Tomorrow, I will leave Germany, I do not like what seems to be coming." And he goes on inventing birds of the strangest kinds. One of these is the little paper bird, which panda bears taught the people of Japan how to make: "But no man has learned to do exactly as the pandas. They say that once they finish making a little paper bird, they place it on their embossed and gracious paws. Then they softly blow on the little bird which comes to life and flies away toward the golden sun of the oriental sky."

In 1956, on his final voyage, before leaving for New Guinea, McCrow writes: "No paper, no pencil, no bincoulars, no compass, no maps, no binnacle, I will not need these this time. I am leaving this unfinished sketch as the only proof of his existence.

I will not waste the little time I have in proving his existence as I am eighty-one years old and no one believes me anymore."

They say he pays for his voyages by doing portraits of children in return for room and board.

Our Relatives

P LENTY OF PEOPLE will say, "I like dogs" or, "I like cats," and then elaborate; cats are independent, dogs are more affectionate, etc. But when they say, "I don't like monkeys," they give no justification. They scrunch up their faces when they say this because monkeys seem too much like us. The resemblance has long been known; a French bishop once said to a chimpanzee: "Speak to me and I shall baptize you." From the same era, another inquiring mind declared: "With a good teacher, he might become a little gentleman."

Only in 1970 was it discovered that bonobos share 98 percent of DNA with humans, and they were then brought into the list of common ancestors: gorilla, orangutan, chimpanzee, and bonobo. (At this very moment, my computer fails to recognize the word *bonobo* and underlines it.) Perhaps this rejection is owed to their likeness to us; the observation of the great understanding exhibited by our ancestors sparks resistance. The indigenous people, who have a clearer sense of everything, call the carayá, or howler monkey (a rowdy and alarmist monkey that can be found from Mexico to Northern Argentina) the "chief of the forest." Félix de Azara says that "carayá" indeed means "chief of the forest."

The greatest resistance against attributing intelligent thought to monkeys comes from linguists and behaviorists. The linguists guard their corner, for even though they have learned to talk, they'll say, "Ah, but with sign language," considering it an inferior form of speech, as if language had come to us from on high and all at once. And the behaviorists believe that monkeys have learned some four hundred words, but only by force of having them hammered in and always with the procurement of some reward. When one of them visited a center for primatological research in the United States, he almost fell down in amazement to see two chimpanzees sitting in the hollow of a tree and meticulously leafing through a magazine; they were carefully turning the pages of books prepared for them with illustrations of food, furniture, etc. And there was no external incentive there, no award for that task.

Today we have set aside the categorical separation between the instinctive and the rational; "instinctive" used to be applied to animals in order to separate instinct from reason and assign the latter to man alone. We now know that many pieces of knowledge are acquired by certain groups, not all; there are local transformations, knowledge acquired only by a particular set. For instance, in Borneo there are orangutans who've been washing their limbs with soap for thirty years; then there are the Japanese macaques (one lone group) who will wash their sweet potatoes before eating them. There's another group, among the Japanese species who will shape balls of snow and then sit on them. There are baboons in Kenya who hunt flamingos and eat them. And though they are not chimpanzees, who stand at the peak of understanding, the rhesus monkeys of India live near houses and markets; when they're going to steal food from a house, they set two watchmen by the door to make sure the way is clear, then they enter through the window, open the freezer, and make their escape loaded down with provisions.

When I was studying philosophy, one discipline was philosophical anthropology. Each philosopher made an effort to consider a prior hypothesis that would support the thesis he or she wished to propose. Man was *Homo faber* for the ability to create tools, *Homo ludens* for childhood play, and so on in succession.

It just so happens that it isn't only primates who fashion tools; ravens do as well. But the intelligence of birds was discovered only a few years ago. Going back to philosophical anthropologists, the one who takes the cake for separating man's intelligence from that of the animal was Max Scheler in his book *The Human Place in the Cosmos*, where he presented man's intelligence as something distinguishable from and inaccessible to all other species, as though it were something fallen from heaven. It's interesting to consider that the thinking concerning both sign language and the fashioning of tools comes from the same mold: "it is not a language like ours, they are not tools like ours," privileging the product obtained over the ability to create. The English school, more gradualist and fonder of observation than categorical divisions, has another point of view. Locke, for example, observed with perplexity that there is no hiatus between animals and plants; there are some unclassifiable specimens, which are like missing links between the two. Charles Darwin goes so far as to say that a person who studies the nature of baboons will do a great deal for metaphysics. Not to mention René Descartes, who considered animals to be programmed machines. It was one of Descartes's disciples who diverged from him regarding animals and said that, with the right professor, they might learn to speak and so become little gentlemen.

Primatology and ethology in general have been held back at times by the prejudices of certain scientists toward colleagues of other nationalities. Japanese primatologists, who've done great work, were discredited by Europeans and Americans because they gave proper names to the chimpanzees, for which they were accused of anthropocentrism. Be that as it may, we have a great deal in common with chimpanzees; they do many things like us. They tickle each other, they laugh. Frans de Waal says of one of them: "I was always impressed by how well Kanzi grasped spoken English." He would obey certain orders: "Put the key in the refrigerator," and "asked to give his doggy a shot, he picks up a plastic syringe and injects it into his stuffed toy dog." And he adds: "Using us as models, these apes spontaneously learn to brush their teeth, ride bicycles, light fires, drive golf carts." And when faced with some conflict because of a decision or a response they must make, they'll scratch their heads just like some of us do. On TV I saw one chimpanzee with hiccups and another heaving a sigh.

POWER AND HARMONY

The quest for power is a distinctive feature of chimpanzee society. Chimpanzees' fights often arise due to the instability of this power; the alpha male's strength is not durable but rather something he must show he's capable of exercising. But the alpha male cannot exercise his power alone; he needs allies, and not just allies, he needs to be recognized by the base. An aspiring usurper of the alpha male will make obvious demonstrations of strength so that no one will doubt his "Here I am." He'll shake and heave branches, moving about noisily, and Frans de Waal says that one candidate for power furnished himself with a few empty kerosene cans and dragged them about, making a great racket. But after so much blowing of his own trumpet, if he isn't accepted by the others, he'll often be expelled from the community as a braggart and a nuisance. Monkeys of high rank have ulcers and heart attacks just like executives—they deal with stress. A male monkey's benefit from being chosen as alpha is that he has a multitude of females available to him. But, for example, a female chimpanzee may prefer to copulate with a monkey of lower rank, and to do so the two must wait until the alpha male is sleeping or else hide from him. The ceremony of mutual grooming, delousing, picking off bits of leaves from their skin serves, among other things, for reconciliation: generally, the one who interacts most with the other monkeys has more power; he grooms many and many groom him. But the interesting thing among chimpanzees is that, in addition to the alpha male, who would be the political leader, the one to lead in offense and defense, there is another important figure: the mediator. This one is selected based on ability to arbitrate in conflicts. The mediator can also be a female, a matriarch. The hierarchy is more stable among the females, for the older ones are stronger than the young. A mediating female will stand between the contenders, one on either side, take them by the hands, and bring the fight to an end. She may end up splitting a branch in half so as to give one piece to each of the ones who'd been fighting over it. Sometimes a male mediator will separate the combatants with his arms, and if one wants to go on fighting, he'll give him a slap. When an alpha male is ousted by another, he'll become depressed, grow pale, cut himself off, withdraw. But if one is injured or unwell in some way, he'll increase his burden of power in order to conceal his weakness and demonstrate his relevance. Chimpanzees can recognize gender and the power plays of humans. De Waal says that some chimpanzees in a zoo in Amsterdam would greet the zoo director very respectfully and with signs of submission; they didn't have daily dealings with him, they had very little contact, yet they showed him the utmost respect every time they saw him.

Among siamang gibbons, both males and females vocalize. From this vocalization, it's possible to perceive not only their whereabouts but also the degree of integration and harmony between the pair. If their song doesn't move to the beat, if they aren't in tune, the neighbors will invade.

Bonobos

De Waal says: "We know little about why bonobos are so different from chimpanzees, but their bloodlines diverged some two million years ago." They stand more erect and are darker and smaller in size; until 1990 they were considered a smaller variety of chimpanzees. Also around 1990 it was discovered that they belong to a matriarchal society; the females are dominant. The females will take a large share of food for themselves and, if they feel like it, toss a bit to the males; other times, they drive them off. Bonobos too know how to distinguish the sexes of humans. Looking at an image of someone they know, they are able to identify a family resemblance. But harmony in the bonobo community comes not through fights over power, as with the chimpanzees, but rather through sex. Sex goes beyond its usual functions; they'll have sex when greeting, when reconciling, when comforting one another. Chimpanzees will reconcile after a fight by kissing and embracing their opponent.

Mirrors and Machinations

Chimpanzees are capable of deceiving the group. A male was observed limping heavily while his aggressor was still present but walking naturally once he was out of view. What's more, they're capable of making false reconciliations and can go through the whole ritual of reconciliation, feigning friendship, only to give the other a snap right after. One Japanese primatologist, Toshisada Nishida, observed a system the males had for getting together with a female without the other males realizing it. These features aren't fixed traits but differ according to region; they aren't innate but acquired behavior, produced in specific social contexts.

But it's not only chimpanzees and bonobos who are capable of deceit; ravens are as well. If they notice they're being observed while hiding some food, they will wait for the voyeur to leave and then hide it somewhere else. And when they approach a stash of hidden food, they keep in mind what the other ravens know. They'll know if their competitors are aware of a place where food is hidden, and, when they perceive that the others have found out about it, they'll try to get there first. And if they're sure the others haven't caught on, they'll approach the spot at a leisurely pace. The raven family, known as the corvids, also includes crows and jays, and all of this was only learned some twenty-five years ago.

If looking at oneself in the mirror is a sign of proto-sentience, it isn't something done only by primates but also some Asian elephants, dolphins, and magpies, another type of corvid. Monkeys will look inside their mouths in the mirror, and the females will turn around to stare at their bottoms; they'll look at injuries, and one monkey who had an ear infection took a little piece of straw, put it into her ear, and ran over to look at herself in the mirror. Right in front of me I have a drawing that de Waal did of a monkey adorning her head with a lettuce leaf, posed as if it were a bow or a hat, and shifting the leaf around while watching herself in the mirror.

INTELLIGENCE AND MEMORY

Monkeys with Down syndrome have been found among both chimpanzees and rhesus macaques. The other monkeys will protect them and allow them to disrespect the alpha male or show off in front of him, for they consider them unimputable. Rhesus macaques have distinct cries for different social situations, and some believe that they can pick up one another's status through these cries. Some bonobos trained in Japan learn language by means of a computer keyboard. But, just as it is with young humans, it often happens that the child learns more than the mother and incorporates new words and concepts; the child learns by seeing how others are taught, in this case the mother.

One bonobo went around with her baby on her back and near

its head a rock she would use to break some other rocks a good distance away. This indicates an idea of foresight, first equipping herself with a tool to be used later. It appears that some monkeys can't stand it if visitors in the zoo insult them (not because they grasp the meaning of an insult but because they understand the body language and the facial expression with which it is delivered). One chimpanzee gathered little rocks in the morning to throw at the people who came in the afternoon. Another case: some young monkeys in captivity were making a great fuss and holding up the delivery of the adult monkeys' dinner; the next day, the monkeys who'd eaten late because of their antics beat them up. Chimpanzees have the capacity to harm others, but this capacity isn't manifested only in its aggressive dimension; it's the flipside of compassion and gratitude. Chimpanzees can cause suffering for their amusement, and I saw one on television playing with an iguana with a mixture of curiosity and sadism very similar to that of humans who subject dogs and cats to rough games. But these anthropoids can take care of a wounded comrade, and they'll gather fruit for their oldest members who can no longer do so. Chimpanzees will comfort their companions with kisses and hugs when they're distressed. Dee Waal says: "Every year when I visit the Burgers' Zoo, in Arnhem, a few chimps still remember me . . . greeting me with excited hooting."

Sometimes animals aren't motivated to perform the tasks imposed on them by people, and it seems chimpanzees get bored quickly and are quite temperamental; later on, from a statistical view, it will be said that such animals did not reach a given standard. It's not that they aren't capable; it's just that they don't feel like learning in that moment. De Waal was working with one elderly female and told her: "Look, I don't have all day," and then she set to work! Why? Because of the nonverbal gestures accompanying the admonition: primates are experts in nonverbal body language. Then there was Georgia, who was in the habit of holding water in her mouth to spew at visitors, and he said to her: "I saw you!" She picked up on several clues to understand what he was saying: he called her by name, held up a finger, and changed his facial expression. She let the water spill out onto the ground.

Behaviorists, who only probe into animals' behavior without taking into account what lies behind it, believe animals live in an eternal present, yet they actually have the capacity not only to remember but to anticipate as well. One chimpanzee would gather warm straw from her cell to later bring outdoors where it was cold. Many chimpanzees will cross great distances carrying branches that they'll whittle down for poking inside beehives or wasp nests. They'll often play games or invent them, and these activities are ones they can expect no reward for but do for pure amusement: one group invented a game that consists of making holes in the ground, filling them up with mud, and stirring them as though preparing some food, a soup or a stew. And like humans, who, to advertise products, will use beautiful people who look like winners as well as those with social prestige, chimpanzees will imitate the behaviors of their group's most prestigious members. These games and certain customs are not instinctive but rather are trends that one individual introduces into the group, thus bringing about local change. The Japanese macaques who wash off their sweet potatoes are one such group.

There's something we humans have lost as a function of our acquisition of language, which privileges communicative content over gesture: we've lost our knowledge of the language of the body, the nonverbal. Not just monkeys, but other mammals and some birds are experts at recognizing this language, which expresses its owner's mood better than a thousand words. De Waal says that when he isn't sure how he's feeling or what mood he's in, he'll take a look at the chimpanzees around him to get out of his confusion. And I myself used to do the same thing with my cat. Whenever I was confused, I'd look at how my cat perceived me and then would know what was happening to me.

First Cousins

I can still remember the bookstore and the moment when I bought Roger Fouts's book, *Next of Kin*. It's a book about chimpanzees with an introduction by Jane Goodall, the famous primatologist. I left the bookshop quite contented and read it all in one shot. It deals with the case of Washoe, the first monkey to have mastered human language through signs. The author's doctoral thesis is based on his experience with Washoe; she will later go on to communicate this language to other monkeys. The thesis student's job was to bathe her, change her diapers, and teach her the language. They'd play peekaboo and another game called "hide baby," in which he would hide her doll. Washoe would make a scene around miniature versions of objects or representations of them, and a car inside a little box caused her such great excitement that she called it "baby," for to her the most pertinent feature was its size. She had two children and lost them; the researchers gave her a child to adopt and she was a caring mother, calling him "baby," but when the little monkey began spitting at people she called him "black bug," which for her was the lowest creature on the social scale. She called her toilet "dirty good" but then extended the word *dirty* to all disagreeable situations, and if Roger was opposed to something she wanted, she'd say, "dirty

Roger." She'd also say "Open food drink," when she wanted to get something from the refrigerator. Though cooperative, she could be imperious at times: when she learned to speak a bit more and saw Roger smoking, she said: "Give me that." And he: "Ask politely." She: "Please give me that hot smoke."

And here she came up with a new theory. When Roger arrived, she said: "Roger hurry, come hug, feed me, gimme clothes, please out, open door." Roger would scare her and the others who followed with an imaginary "black dog" if they were making a big fuss, and then they'd go still and silent. Chimpanzees can talk about and understand something that isn't present, and Roger would tell Washoe and her friends stories in which they were the protagonists. Roger Fouts says that, despite what behaviorists believe (that monkeys act based on reward response), they will do many things without expecting any reward, like talking about foods or visitors' appearances. Washoe was even capable of blackmailing the students who drove her around, threatening to smash the windows of the car if they didn't buy her a coke. She believed that she belonged to the human race. (She hadn't seen other monkeys since a very young age.) When several new additions arrived to take part in the sign-language group, the ethologist asked Washoe what they were, and she said "black bugs." But when referring to Thelma, another female monkey, she called her "black woman." And when some others arrived and Washoe had already interacted with them, she threw herself into the water to save another female monkey, whom she didn't know, from drowning.

Washoe also understood the family ties between Roger and his wife, and when the couple's six-year-old daughter was leaving, Roger asked Washoe who she was and she said: "Roger Debbi baby." Washoe had established the difference between *them* and *us*. *Us* was the world of people, herself included, and *them* comprised dogs, cats, and black bugs. And when she reached sexual maturity, she'd fall in love with doctoral students and kiss her one of choice. She'd call a swan "water bird."

LUCY

Lucy was raised in a family like a human being, slept in the same bed as her human parents, and perceived herself as human. She had a cat whom she wanted to teach to speak using sign language; she was overprotective of her; the cat would go and take shelter up in a tree but she'd run out looking for her and get her down. When she accidentally injured her cat, her human parents berated her for it, and she said: "Sorry hurt." Lucy would drink tea from the kettle, filling it up with water and putting it on the stove, getting a teabag from the cupboard and preparing it. While she lived with her adoptive parents, she'd sneak out to steal things from the kitchen if they were away, and she explored her vagina using various objects; once she even plugged in the vacuum cleaner and applied it to her genital area. She was always asking to be comforted and making a scene in front of her parents so they would feel sorry for her, but as soon as they were out of view she'd change her expression. Lucy paired her dinner with wine and loved the TV.

OTHERS

Moya liked red dresses, she'd put on makeup and look at herself in the mirror, she'd try to seduce everyone, she was the first to approach the volunteers who came to care for her, she'd brush her hair in front of them.

Ally, like Lucy, was a chimpanzee raised by humans who knew sign language, and she wound up on the island where Washoe and the other chimpanzees were living. When Washoe approached Ally and spoke to him in sign language, he stood there petrified. The ethologist says: "The way you might if you encountered a talking dog." He went crazy after this contact, pulling out his hair and refusing to eat, until he finally understood that he was one of them.

Washoe would clean the floor with soapy water and a brush, knew how to unclog the toilet when it got clogged, and would test the volunteers by asking them to give her ice cream when she knew they couldn't. To choose candidates to look after them while he was away, Roger opted for a convenient and clever device: he let them take charge of the selection themselves; the monkeys would spit on the ones they didn't like.

The chimpanzees were able to completely dismantle a woven wire fence and did so in the absence of any caretakers or guardians. Due to a lack of resources for maintaining the property, the animals had to allow paid visits; when the visitors left, the chimpanzees would make comments about their outfits, their bald spots, their beards, the Band-Aids they had over cuts, etc. One rainy day, Tatu wanted to go outside and a volunteer told her: "Sorry very cold." She replied: "Give clothes me."

A FEW INCIDENTS

It seems to me that the work of a primatologist, ornithologist, or ethologist in general contributes to our understanding of man as a natural being, with no qualitative difference from the primates who begot him. Fortunately, we've moved beyond the conception of instinct as something blind and mechanical. One anthropologist studied the use of medicinal plants among chimpanzees; a human group in Africa follows these chimpanzees on their medicinal quests. Instinct or intelligence? The concept of intelligence as refined instinct favors the perception of nuances, gradations, and not absolutes. People say "base instincts" and "high ideals." The scheme of "civilization and barbarism" has the same assumptions: there was only one idea of civilization in the nineteenth century, all other ways of life were barbarism. Racism perceives one race as being absolutely distinct from another, and it makes me happy to confirm that the majority of biologists in the nineteenth century weren't racists. Humboldt loved the United States but objected to the institution of slavery and likewise the colonialism of European countries. William McCrow, ornithologist, now at the start of the twentieth century, objected to Great Britain for its possession of colonies and traveled around the world pursuing birds and fleeing from the warmongering Europeans. Fouts, says: "Most people who espouse human superiority don't realize that their view stems from the same ancient idea that produced nineteenth-century racism."

SOUTHERN SCREAMER

The Horco Molle Nature Reserve

THE HORCO MOLLE Nature Reserve is near downtown in San Miguel de Tucumán. I go with Marcela Canelada and Martín Castagnet. The animals are on parcels of land so vast, green, and wooded that I now wish I had a garden like some creatures do, with so many plants and that kind of square footage. Biologists, veterinarians, and rangers work there caring for injured or abandoned animals that people sometimes pick up on the side of the road and bring to them. In other cases, people keep them on the patios of their houses as if they were dogs and cats, and they'll abandon them or bring them to the reserve when they grow tired of them or realize they can't keep them as pets anymore. For instance, they'll keep a rhea or a seriema, a large gray bird that looks like an inflated turkey, as a pet. On their patios they'll also keep foxes on leashes and baby pumas. When the puma grows up, he goes for the neck with his teeth, while a rhea will go for the eyes. People even keep armadillos as pets, housing them inside dog crates. They'll donate capuchin monkeys because they're a danger to the home. They imitate everything a person does, and if someone uses a knife . . . they will follow suit. That must be the origin of the saying "More dangerous than a monkey with a razor."

The first thing we saw as soon as we arrived was an operation being done on the wing of a variable hawk, which lay out on a large table that must also serve as the place for breakfast and *tertulia*. The hawk was asleep, anesthetized, with his little legs crossed. Flavia Rodríguez is a biologist now doing her doctorate, and her dissertation is on brocket deer; everyone here specializes on a single animal. She says: "Brockets (*guazubirá*) are very sensitive to noise, and they're in a partial-freedom area and can be put in with the peccaries." (I was hoping they'd have elective affinities, but no.) "Peccaries are very aggressive, even among themselves, and capuchin and howler monkeys are in partial freedom as well. In that area are the red-footed tortoises, which have spots of color; the indigenous people considered those tortoises to have been painted."

We take a guided tour with Paola Alberti, a biology student and wildlife ranger. I ask her:

"Can animals recognize their caretakers?"

"They don't like the veterinarians because they anesthetize them, handle them, etc. They do like us rangers. We did several experiments, putting balls, toys, and boxes in to see what each animal would do with them. Instead of giving the monkeys their food in a container, we put it inside sealed bottles. The female monkey in charge opened it first and then the others followed suit, though I don't know if it was because they'd seen her actions and realized the method or because she gave them permission."

And I think that these reasons go hand in hand; the one in charge is the one with the knowledge, something often assumed among people. Marcela takes over: "We put in a tambourine up there for the howler monkey who's always way up in the trees and he plays it."

In the reserve there is a mountain turkey, a mountain fox, and a mountain wildcat, as they are known here. The fox came from a house, for despite being wild, he still follows people. His tail is thick and silky as though someone brushed it every day. He keeps pacing back and forth, always along the same route; it's a confinement syndrome: biologists call it "stereotypic movement." Marcela says: "They're almost pests; they eat chickens, and people will put one on a leash like a dog." The wildcat is like an ordinary cat but taller and more elegant, and they're kept as pets too. And Marcela relates something curious: the turkey that's visible up in a tree is visited every day by a member of the same species who lives in a house. Could they be friends? Farther along, there are several armadillo burrows, but the armadillos don't show themselves; they come out at night. They too are pets, and dogs will bite their tails; reattaching an armadillo's tail is a common operation. They're fed wet dog food, that's how they hydrate. Then we saw the plush-crested jay, which is a corvid and therefore quite intelligent; she steals food from the monkey, who gets irritated and growls. The jay imitates the sounds of other birds and anything else it hears, for example, the buzzing of an electric fence. Paola says: "My boss tried to trick her, but it's useless, she won't fall for it."

The brocket deer are a pair and come from a house, where they lived in the yard as pets. They're quite little; they look pre-adolescent, and they're very sensitive to all of the noise in their surroundings, like that of airplanes, even getting spooked by the lawn mower. The rangers put collars on them to monitor them and follow their movements. In the partial-freedom area there's also the puma, donated by a family; their lifespan is usually around twenty years. The one here is eighteen and has spent half his life on the reserve, and they can't set him free because he doesn't know how to hunt. (The test they do before releasing an animal is to verify that it can hunt; they toss in a mouse, but the puma just stares and doesn't catch it.) They must know how to defend themselves as well, otherwise they'd fall prey to the first hunter. All of this made me think of two things: first the reserve's protectionist attitude, since they will dutifully care for animals who aren't fit for the outside world for many years, and then the rigid stance that existed some years ago, separating instinct from intelligence so categorically. If instinct were a constant, it would be reactivated within the animal in the presence of new, adverse situations. Instead, newer theories confirm significant modifications in animal behavior that can be seen in the existence of fashions, as when certain groups of monkeys—not all of them— have the habit of meticulously washing their bodies.

That puma we saw here has confinement syndrome, going back and forth along the same path all the time. From far away we saw a tapir; people eat their meat. They say it's similar to that of a horse. And then we saw the Darwin's rhea, a bit smaller than the standard rhea. Paola says: "When he's about to attack, he spreads his wings to make himself bigger. He's the one we're most afraid of here on the reserve. He goes right for the eyes. We wear masks to approach him. A guard had his hand seriously injured."

We return to downtown San Miguel along Calle Mate de

Luna. Martín bought a book on Argentine birds for his grandmother, and Marcela got me a postcard of a spider monkey. He has an interesting fringe of hair and eyes luminous as though newly unveiled.

Plaza Almagro

H ERE WE ARE in winter, but the winter has made a mistake: it's a spring day. The plaza is full of dogs, alone and accompanied; they've been set loose to enjoy the lovely day. Beside me sits a very circumspect lady with a dog on A+ behavior, not even sparing a look at the dogs in the pen as they bark wildly. She says to me:

"I've always protected animals. Back when I worked at a logistics warehouse I used to pick up all the ones that people dumped there."

"Señora, what do they store at a logistics warehouse?"

"What does that matter? I have great memories of Torolo and Negrita, who'd made a hole in the concrete to hide their puppies, and Torolo used to slip away and come back later, always right at mealtime."

When she says Torolo's name, her voice makes it sound as though he were some famous singer.

A girl walks by with a slightly frenzied dog, and the lady says, "To have contact with a dog, you need to be balanced, and if the dog has a lot of energy, you keep yours low. That girl is adding to her dog's energy."

I am afraid I won't pass the energy or aptitude test and go off to another bench, whistling softly to myself. There sits María Cristina, with her little dog Sharka. The dog is wearing a jacket on which it says "Playboy." María Cristina has something birdlike and nocturnal about her, with her lips in a shade of blue; her hair is golden, and she wears tinted glasses. She says:

"They gave her to me with the name Sharka. She came from a house with an abusive man, he'd beat the people and the dogs. My sister feeds her on pork chops and roast chicken, and we give her apples, that's right. She's the first dog I've ever had. At home we had canaries, finches, parakeets. In my family, we're the kind to be around animals. In our house the birds would fly loose around the kitchen and then voluntarily get into their cages on their own."

At one end of the plaza, a dog is running beside his owner, big blockheads the pair of them. The dog doesn't know whether to play with the ball his owner is throwing, chase the pigeons, or go after the other dogs. The owner has a similar appearance, and, as though exaggerating his feeling of heat, he has on a sleeveless T-shirt; he seems to be sweating profusely, and he gives me the impression that he's pursuing several careers or taking on various jobs but never sticking to any, always being drawn to something new. It's like Torolo's owner said: if our energies are overlapping, we don't do well.

But it's spring . . . On another bench sits Victoria, but she has to go. She says:

"He goes by Luis, but his real name is Luis Alberto, after Spinetta."

Farther along sits Mariela, age somewhere around twenty. She seems as fragile as her clothing, which is in varying colors but looks as if it's been washed with bleach or some corrosive liquid that has left all of the colors completely faded. For the same reason her skirt had a hole in it and is made of wool as fine as a strand of spittle.

"It that your dog?"

"No, he's my friend's. I feel like he's free inside the plaza."

"And what's his name?"

"Why should he have just one name? He goes by Teo or Cielo. No, I don't want to own a dog, because pets are possessions—we decide when they can go out or how much they eat. I don't want to enslave a living being. People even determine where they can sleep, they have to sleep wherever others decide."

"And is there a reason for that austere outfit you're wearing?"

"No, just for the ensemble of colors."

"Ah. And where would you like to live?"

"In the country. I'd like to be a rural teacher, but I also like trades like carpentry, cooking. . ."

"Would you keep animals in the country?"

"I'd like to have a dog without a leash, free. I'd let him be with other animals…"

"And if your dog ran away, would you go looking for him?"

"I'd go looking for him, but I'm not convinced that he'd ever come back."

I leave the realm of freedom and go over to the pen, which is the realm of barking. I go in and dogs of all sizes come over, leaping up on me; a dog walker energetically gets them in line, though I don't know if Mariela would have approved of this exercising of authority. The walker's name is Ramón, and he's short on temper and few on words. He doesn't feel like talking about the dogs; one is called Vicky, another Néstor. Named for Kirchner. (A girl I once asked for directions had named her dogs Fidel and Sandino.) Ramón says:

"I've always had a pepé, because purebred dogs are very choosy about their food."

"What's a pepé?"

"It's a mutt," he says, and pays me no more mind. He doesn't feel like talking.

Walking along the gravel path, I come across Iván, from Corrientes, a chamamé singer. He knows a lot about dogs; his is Juanita. He says:

"She inherited the personality of a bloodhound from her father, and her mother comes from a bulldog and terrier mix. We've committed barbarities with animals by turning them into spectacles, like in bullfighting or cockfights."

"Does your dog know when she's misbehaving?"

"Yes, when she makes a mess, she gets onto the futon and doesn't move. She's five months old. Sometimes she'll tear a pillowcase. And she resents it when I leave, like a cat. Yesterday I had to run an errand and it took a while, and when I came back, she gave me the cold shoulder."

"What kind of thing do you sing?"

"I'm a chamamé musician, I write poetry; poetry seeks you out, just like dogs."

I go back to the pen once more, and there's a completely new line-up of dogs, and here's Nicolás, a walker. He studied to be a park ranger in Buenos Aires; he's from Lobos and in the future aspires to become a ranger in a protected area and study the fauna.

"What about dogs drew your attention when you started working?"

"My attention was drawn to the way they communicated with the posture of their bodies and the energy they transmit. The energy thing stands out. I have a friend who's a walker, and the dog that leads her pack is the tiniest one. They express things with their bodies that we can't. I think they're more honest than we are."

I don't want to get myself into those complex depths, so I ask:

"Why do tiny dogs confront much larger dogs? Can't they perceive their size?"

"Little dogs want to demonstrate their energy. I think they perceive energy more than size."

"What do you remember from your first days as a dog walker?"

"The pack concept: I would end up being the alpha, but some packs have an alpha and a beta, that is, not just a first but also a second, though not all packs do. I come from Lobos, and I've seen a street dog curled up from the cold, and when another dog nearby growls, the curled up one will stretch out in a show of submission, all without physical contact. One thing that alarms lots of dogs is a hat with earflaps (if a man is wearing one). They can't understand it, maybe because the ears are hidden, and they're also disturbed by fluorescent colors, but they always look at what people have on their heads."

"And what surprises them the most?"

"They're shocked if someone hits them because that behavior doesn't happen among them; they bite each other, they don't hit."

"And what's your dog's name?"

"My dog comes from Lobos. His name is Lennon."

Then he tells me how European hares and starlings are threatening the local species, but that comes from his knowledge as a park ranger.

And I go off to take a look at someone on a bench; I'm puzzled by her mater dolorosa bearing. She has a puppy on her skirt who is very comfortable in that spot but wears a mournful and expectant expression.

"Is he yours?"

"No, he got lost here in the plaza. They say he belongs to some people who come here often."

"What's his name?"

"He doesn't have a name. I don't know."

"So you aren't going to keep him?"

"I wish I could, but I live in a hotel."

And the girl comes to the plaza every day, in case the owner turns up.

CHECKERED WOODPECKER

Oddities

IN THE JUNGLES of Borneo there are pygmy species of bears, elephants, and rhinoceroses too. The rhinoceros is a descendent of the enormous woolly rhino, which lived on the earth millions of years ago. There are also miniature horses and diminutive monkeys. And there are winged lizards in Borneo as well: they spread their wings with a mechanical movement, and off they fly. There are fish and squirrels that fly: their wings developed during the Ice Age. In Borneo too live proboscis monkeys, and it's unknown what purpose such a long nose could serve. I don't think there's any need to search around so much; that's how they come, it is what it is. These monkeys, unlike others, can swim very well. And they call a red-faced monkey the "English monkey," after the color that white people turn when they get too much sun. In Borneo there's a jumping fish that can leap two meters above the water's surface to eat insects. There's also an armadillo that will swim to get out of his burrow when it floods. How can he do it with those stubby little feet?

In the Amazon there are water lilies (giant water hyacinths) that will grow twenty-five centimeters per day. A caiman can sunbathe on one of them. The jaguar is the only feline that swims. There they go with those big paws. And the brown bear too will plunge into the water to fish.

As for the education of young, cheetahs will hunt tiny prey and release them close to the cubs so they will get to know the prey. And an elephant herd will pause so the baby elephants can catch up.

In the Amazon there are otters and giant tortoises, which can reach a meter in length and weigh ninety kilos; the otters reach two meters in length, and maybe that's where the Brazilians get their expression, "O mais grande do mundo." Sloths only come down to the ground once a week to defecate.

On the Russia-China border, a turtle crossed from China to Russia by way of a lake; she hunts herons and is capable of fighting a crocodile. It's quite curious to see a trampling turtle.

The ever-vigilant prairie dogs, seeing a snake approach, will designate one (who knows which they choose for such a task) to face it down, and the poor thing gives his body, his cries and warnings.

There's a bear who eats flowers and scratches his body up against a tree. He wears an expression of great happiness; I'd like to try both of those things.

How strange is life upon the earth.

The Rolinga Dog

I MET SEÑORA ESTELA in the street as her dog dragged her along, leading her in a zigzag; I observed it happening and we struck up a conversation. She told me she'd been quite athletic from age ten until ten years ago: I asked if we could do an interview another day, sitting someplace quiet. The dog had on a onesie with some lettering.

"What's that lettering? Is it for a soccer team?"

"No, it's for the Rolling Stones; she's a Rolinga."

A few short days later, sitting in a Havanna Café, Estela tells me about her life as well as the dog's.

"I practiced boxing, judo, taekwondo, karate, fencing (that one I wasn't so good at). I was the equestrian champion of Argentina, starting at age ten, and I broke ponies. At home we had lots of animals; I was comfortable around them. Papá had a monkey who used to masturbate whenever I was sick; it was because of the smell, and if you put on perfume, same deal. We took him to the zoo because we couldn't keep him in the house any longer, and when we left him there, he was spying on us, hidden behind a newspaper in his cage. It was really funny. It looked like he was reading. He used to do it in the house too. Also, my husband and I got a sailboat and sailed around the coast of Uruguay and Brazil. I'm most comfortable with animals, sports, the water."

"What's the little doggy's name?"

"Her name is Ashakis, which means 'pretty' in Egyptian. I called the other one Yuyú, but she took no notice if people called her by that name. She chose her own name, because when we went to the Arabic center a boy said 'Inshallah' to her and she responded right away, so she ended up Isha."

"Why so many Arabic or Egyptian names?"

"I have an Arabic grandmother, and I adopted the Islamic faith, though I'm pantheistic. I believe everything has life; a stone has life, and if treated well an animal will much later go on to become a person. I have a large chest completely filled with Egyptian objects. Isha the dog and Moro the cat died within a very short period of time." (She shows me a photo of them on her phone.) "They'd get up there. Isha was a rocker. I'm going to say something esoteric, many people don't believe me, but I can see lights shining up above, and I believe it's them, that they're present, even in absence. I studied Arabic but later gave it up. They kept the women separate from the men or sent us to the back; Arab men believe they have rights over women."

"What kind of relationship does Ashakis have with you and with other dogs?"

"If I have any resentment toward a person, she'll growl at them. If my husband touches me affectionately, she'll get agitated and growl at him. She gets along well with other dogs, but they're afraid of her since she plays pretty rough. For instance Trapito, the one at the tire shop, he sees her coming and hides."

"Where does she sleep?"

"Pressed up against me with her little feet. If I stir she goes to my husband's bed, and when she thinks I've dozed off, she comes back. Whenever we come in from the street I wash her feet, her muzzle, and her tail."

"What words does she understand or obey?"

"When Isha was alive, I was studying Portuguese, and I'd say words to her in Portuguese and she'd understand. I spoke to her in Arabic and Italian too. She was amazing." She smiles. "To me, it's like they're extraterrestrials observing us all the time."

"Can you distinguish between different tones in their barks?"

"Sure, when people on my floor go to take the elevator down, she'll bark loudly, with lots of power. At night, before bed, around nine thirty, she barks in a different way; she steals the pillows and wants to play. There's another bark for when she stands by the window grate, barking at cars" (a cell phone photo of the dog up on two feet, her front paws gripping the grate, in an attentive stance).

"Have you ever put on a TV show with dogs or other animals to see if she'd look at them?"

"Yes, some people don't want to believe me, but my girls watch that show with César, the dog trainer, and others with dogs in them. I once had a cat, and as soon as she heard the music from *Me llaman Gorrión*, the telenovela, remember it?, she'd come running to look at the little birds."

"What kind of things do you say to her?"

"'Give your mamma a kiss. Come here and give it to me.' I had a dog who thought my ear was a nipple, and she'd tug and tug at it."

"Have you ever dreamed about your dogs?"

"The dogs, no, but I used to have Siamese kittens. My mother had senile dementia and kicked one of them pretty hard; I took him to the vet but he didn't make it. I started dreaming about him every night and even saw him here, by day. It went on for a month like that until the cat said 'Let me go, let me go,' and then I didn't dream about him anymore."

"I'd like you to tell me about the baby outfits they're wearing."

"They aren't baby clothes; they're these lovely capes, each one made according to the animal's own style. Isha had clothes like a biker, a rocker, a leather jacket with studs and a badge. The current one has more military-style clothing. I've made little capes for her, she has something like twenty. She wears a rhinestone collar. Where do I buy them? In Plaza Francia. I also dressed her up as the devil for Halloween." (It's on the phone; the dog has a kind of crown of fire glowing around her head, and it looks like two lit-up deer antlers.) "I bought her a camo jacket like the ones from the army, green, black, and tan; she has blankets with patches from the Russian army. Where can you buy that? In Parque Centenario. She has a Rolinga cape with the tongue from the Stones and a summer hat for going to the plaza in the sun."

As we leave, we come across her husband, who's out taking the dog for a walk. She says:

"Let's pretend we don't see her and see what she does."

But as we get closer, her husband waves and the dog notices her. She says:

"Give your mamma a kiss, *preciosa*."

And the dog sticks out her long tongue and runs it over the woman's mouth and nose.

LAPWING